"I want a baby."

Ty stepped back a pace, stunned. "What does that have to do with me?"

"I want you to give me a child."

Ty blinked, took in Jade's very serious expression. "That's a pretty good tactic, beautiful. You nearly gave me heart failure. But I'm not falling for it, so move your sweet little buns away from that door. My brothers need me."

She shook her head. "I want a baby, and you're the man who can help me."

He smiled, staggered by her charming ploy to keep him in the bunkhouse. "Well, of course I can help you. But as we both know, I'm leaving. I don't have time for romance and nonsense, and I'm not getting married so—"

"I didn't say I wanted to marry you," Jade said. "You're never coming back to Bridesmaids Creek, so you're the perfect man for what I need."

THE SEAL'S
HOLIDAY BABIES

BY
TINA LEONARD

® and ™ are trademarks owned and used by the trademark owner and/or its licensee. Trademarks marked with ® are registered with the United Kingdom Patent Office and/or the Office for Harmonisation in the Internal Market and in other countries.

Published in Great Britain 2014
by Mills & Boon, an imprint of Harlequin (UK) Limited,
Eton House, 18-24 Paradise Road, Richmond, Surrey, TW9 1SR

© 2014 Tina Leonard

ISBN: 978-0-263-91335-4

23-1114

Harlequin (UK) Limited's policy is to use papers that are natural, renewable and recyclable products and made from wood grown in sustainable forests. The logging and manufacturing processes conform to the legal environmental regulations of the country of origin.

Printed and bound in Spain
by CPI, Barcelona

Tina Leonard is a *USA TODAY* bestselling and award-winning author of more than fifty projects, including several popular miniseries for the Mills & Boon® Cherish™ line. Known for bad-boy heroes and smart, adventurous heroines, her books have made the *USA TODAY*, Waldenbooks, Ingram and Nielsen BookScan bestseller lists. Born on a military base, Tina lived in many states before eventually marrying the boy who did her crayon printing for her in the first grade. You can visit her at www.tinaleonard.com, and follow her on Facebook and Twitter.

Many thanks to the wonderful readers who embrace
my work so loyally—I can never thank you enough.

Chapter One

"Hang on a sec," Ty Spurlock said to Sheriff Dennis McAdams, stunned as he watched a tall redhead wearing seriously tight blue jeans that complemented her seriously sexy figure walk into The Wedding Diner on the arm of Sam Barr, a bachelor recruit whom Ty had brought to town for the express purpose of matchmaking.

It appeared that a match might indeed be in the making. The problem was, the redhead wasn't one of Ty's intended bachelorettes.

Because he secretly had his eye on her for himself.

"What was that?" Ty demanded.

"What was what?"

"Jade Harper going into The Wedding Diner with Sam."

Dennis grinned at him. "Free country, isn't it?"

"Sure it is." Ty sank onto the hood of the sheriff's cruiser and pondered why the idea of Jade and Sam together bothered him, like a real bad toss from a bull. He'd had those, many of those. They were never any fun.

Neither was this. "Is there something going on there I don't know about?"

Dennis's eyes twinkled. "Do you *think* there's something you should you know about? Are you taking over from Madame Matchmaker, our resident maker of matches? That'll put Cosette's pink-frosted hair in a twist for sure, if she thinks you're butting in on her area of expertise."

Ty felt strongly that Sheriff Dennis might be keeping something from him, which only made Ty resolve to get to the bottom of the matter. Jade had no business going out with Sam Barr, as prime for matchmaking as Sam might be. "*Is* there something going on between Sam and Jade?"

Dennis shook his head. "You'll have to ask Jade. Or Sam."

The sheriff was being deliberately obtuse, prickling him because he could. Nobody understood him the way Dennis did. The man had been elected sheriff after Ty's adoptive father, Terence, had given up the sheriff's job—fifteen years of being a great sheriff undone by one rumor. A rumor that had never gone away. But Sheriff Dennis had always supported Terence Spurlock, and Ty appreciated that more than he could say. Maybe only another sheriff could understand how loose lips and bad information could strike down a career and a man. "Or I could just ask you, since nothing goes on in Bridesmaids Creek that gets past you."

Dennis chuckled. "True enough."

"So? Is there?" Ty asked impatiently.

Dennis crossed his arms and smiled. "Didn't you bring those four cowboys here to find them brides? Sam Barr, Squint Mathison, Justin Morant and Francisco Rodriguez Olivier Grant, otherwise known as Frog?"

"What does that have to do with Jade?"

Dennis laughed. "Ty, you can't blame her for dating

someone. Jade thinks you don't know she's alive, except for her occasionally scooping you some ice cream in her mother's shop. You haven't exactly pursued her."

Ty grunted, glancing around the main square of the town he called home, even as an adopted son, and the town to which he owed so much. Owed them everything because they'd helped raise him, and because he'd had a great childhood because of them.

He owed them everything but his bachelorhood.

"Is there a problem?" Dennis asked.

"No." There was, but he knew Dennis wouldn't needle him about it further. Except he did.

"You could always try talking to her," he said, surprising Ty. Dennis prodded him in a gentle, fatherly way that made him miss his own dad.

"I'm good at talking," Ty said, "but I'm a couple weeks away from trying to make it into the SEALs. I have nothing to offer Jade." He'd be gone for six long months of training, and then a little longer, if he made it.

No. When *I make it.*

Mentally, he reviewed The Plan, which was so far working like a charm.

Bring home eligible, trustworthy, elementally studly bachelors with the intent of pressing some of the ladies— not Jade—into marriage. This would start a rollerball of reactions: namely, babies and families, new blood in Bridesmaids Creek.

Which was very important in a town that was one step away from dying off completely.

He wasn't about to let that happen. No, everything was working smoothly, with Mackenzie Hawthorne and her four darling little girls now married to rodeo rider Justin Morant. That was the beauty of goals and plans—

they worked like charms because they were road signs pointing the way to the future. One needed merely to stick to a plan and not deviate; that was the key.

Victims number two, three and four—those being Sam, Frog and Squint—were certainly catnip to the many ladies in town. So there was no reason under the clear blue sky of Bridesmaids Creek, Texas, that Sam should settle on Jade Harper.

"Eat your heart out much?" Sheriff Dennis asked, jarring him back to the present.

"I'm fine."

"I think Jade would understand the whole BUD/S training thing, Ty. She's an independent girl. She works hard. Don't you think it might be better to speak than to hold your tongue to the point that you lose her forever?"

Lose her forever? Ty chewed on that a moment. He wasn't going to lose Jade, because he'd never had Jade. What he had was The Plan. Nothing could disrupt it, because you didn't get into the SEALs by being an indecisive doorknob. You accomplished that by having determination and focus, and by serving one master. And the only way to clear his father's name, to rebuild the Spurlock brand, was to return home a man of his word. The people of BC—Bridesmaids Creek—had ceased believing that Terence Spurlock was a man of his word when a stranger to BC had been allegedly murdered at the local haunted house, the Hanging H, Mackenzie Hawthorne's place. Folks said Terence had been bought off by the town's evil shyster in big boots, Robert Donovan, who owned significant chunks of town and was determined to own more, carving it up into retail parcels that enriched his considerable wealth. If he could get the Hawthornes to sell, along with the owners of the ranches surrounding Jade's place, Donovan would have the kingdom he desired. But because the people had mostly grouped together against him, refusing to sell, Donovan currently held smaller, disconnected and farther-flung chunks of land not suitable for his grand visions.

Ty's father would never have been bought off by anyone. It burned Ty's gut that some folks—not everyone, but enough—had put such a rumor out there. More than anything, he hated that Bridesmaids Creek was held hostage by Robert Donovan and his coterie of greedy swindlers.

"I understand the mission," Dennis said softly. "I'm just saying you don't have to pay for what happened to your father by losing something you love dearly."

Ty moved away from the voice of temptation, which was intended to be the voice of reason. Sheriff Dennis was a good man. He wanted to help. When Ty's father had died of a broken heart from losing the town's trust—and Ty was sure as the setting sun that that's what had driven his father to his grave—Dennis had been there to remind him of what a very good man his father had been.

Ty clapped Dennis on the back and walked in the opposite direction from The Wedding Diner—and Jade.

"It's a dumb idea," Ty said a half hour later, relenting on entering The Wedding Diner, because his curiosity was killing him. He inserted himself at the table in The Wedding Diner with his buddies Squint and Frog so he had an excellent visual on Jade and Sam, but whether he was torturing himself on purpose he couldn't say. "In fact, that idea is so dumb it makes me wonder if you've poured something strong in your coffee."

Squint shrugged. "You don't want a family. We do."

Frog nodded. "You brought us to BC to find women. We want what Justin got when he married Mackenzie. He got a family."

Ty swallowed, not about to admit that the idea was very appealing. "You wouldn't know what to do with Justin's four babies."

"I don't care how many babies are involved," Squint said, sipping his coffee thoughtfully. "I just care that babies are eventually involved."

"So let me get this straight. You're going to propose pregnancy to a couple of ladies. Not marriage, just pregnancy."

"That about sums it up." Frog eyed with pleasure the plate of steaming eggs, toast and bacon a waitress set down in front of him. "Women aren't looking for a ring anymore, Ty. They want to know that the man they choose can give them a family. And personally, I want to know that I have children in my future. So it's a win-win."

"We're not saying we couldn't love a woman who didn't want children," Squint said. "But we think Justin's got a pretty good setup, and it inspires us. Plus we're pretty good father candidates."

Ty grunted. "Have you chosen your victims?" This ought to be rich. He couldn't wait to hear more details from men whom he'd specifically brought here for the very purpose of finding brides and making families to grow BC.

Just not in the manner in which they were planning to go about it.

"Well, Sam's picked Jade," Squint said, nodding his head in the redhead's direction. "That's as far as we've gotten."

Ty winced. If Sam thought he could just propose pregnancy to an independent woman like Jade Harper, it might be worth hanging around to see him get handed his head. Ty almost laughed at Sam's plan.

Then again, maybe it wasn't that funny. What if Jade said yes? She was twenty-seven, and a beauty like her shouldn't still be on the market, except she claimed she wasn't ready to settle down.

That might be changing now that her best friend, Mackenzie, was happily married.

Ty shrugged off the vague sense of uneasiness the thought gave him. "Picking a lady and having her fall for you are two different things." He glanced Jade's way, commanded himself to quit staring.

"We thought you'd support our plan," Squint said, his tone surprised. "When you lured us to BC, you said there were plenty of ladies looking to settle down. When you've been in the military as long as we were, the thought of ladies looking to settle down is pretty inviting."

"Yeah, why are you beefing about this?" Frog glared at him. "Dude, if you have a better idea, speak up. If not, say nothing. You're leaving soon enough, and you won't be doing much communicating once you're trying to get through BUD/S. So our story won't be of much interest to you."

In other words, butt out. "Your plan is fine. Fool-hardy, but fine. I wish you all the best." A horrible thought occurred to Ty. "What if Jade were to say yes to Sam's stupid pregnancy idea?"

His two friends/hires/tricksters stared at him.

"Well, they'd get married," Frog said. "As sure as my name is Francisco Rodriguez Olivier Grant, I'd probably be best man."

"That would be me," Squint said, "as sure as my name's John Squint Mathison."

It could be serious if his lunkheaded buddies were already scrabbling over who was going to get high honor at this imaginary wedding. *What possible difference does it make to me? Free country, like Dennis said.*

He sneaked another glance at Jade, all long and lean and capable and sexy, with a mop of burgundy-red hair that was a siren's call to Ty. She had a bright smile that teased, always laughing at him, and somehow with him. Captivating him. A laugh that never failed to bring a smile of response to his face, no matter what his mood was. No, when he'd thought up The Plan, the plan of bringing life back to BC, he'd put Jade on a pedestal out of sight, in a mental closet marked Private. Do Not Touch.

Mine.

Sam put his big, beefy hand over Jade's delicate one, and Ty could hear that musical laugh across the aisle, reaching his ears with a pang that lodged in his heart. Something blew in his brain, like a transformer struck by lightning, and the next thing he knew, he was sliding into the white booth occupied by Jade and Sam, tucking himself up against Jade in the most friendly, brotherly fashion, because she expected friendly and brotherly from him.

Only he knew it was more of an ambush.

JADE GRINNED AT Ty when he bumped in next to her, jostling her arm away from Sam's. "Look at you," she said to Ty. "All buzz cut and ready to report for duty."

Ty palmed his newly shorn head. She'd loved his hair long and wild, but he looked just as hot with it short, too. That was the problem with a rascal like Ty—he *looked* irresistible shaved or wild and woolly.

Spiritually, he was way too woolly for her.

"I let one of the ladies buzz me down," Ty said, and Sam grinned.

"Your mother took the sheep shears to him," Sam said.

"Betty didn't have sheep shears," Ty said, "but believe me, she was determined the brass wouldn't be disappointed with me when I showed up for training."

"It's short." Jade smiled. "I can just imagine Mom giving you the treatment. In another world, she could have been a hairstylist. The ice-cream shop just happened to get to her first."

"A remarkable woman," Sam agreed, and Ty elbowed Jade so that she looked at him again.

"Did you just elbow me? In a brotherly, somewhat obnoxious way?"

He looked pained. "I'm not really your brother. As much as it felt like that growing up, I'm not exactly brotherly material, as has been well noted by just about everyone."

Including her, which was why she kept Ty very much on the outskirts of her radar. "Mom practically raised you, along with everyone else in this town. You even had a bunk at our place." Her gaze softened as she took in Ty's square, determined jaw and wide brown eyes. "You broke a lot of noses for my sake when we were growing up."

Sam laughed. "He tried to break everything when

we were on the circuit. Now go away, *brother.* This is a private lunch."

"Private?" Ty glared at Sam. "Nothing's private in BC."

"This is," Jade said. "You have to take your overprotective, buttinsky self elsewhere."

She hated to send him off. But the thing about Ty was that the more he hung around her, the more her hopes rose. It was something she had almost no control over. He treated her like a little sister—and her heart mooned for him. Stupidly.

And this year, her resolution was to get on with her life and accept that Ty was simply too much bad boy for her. Her practical nature knew this, accepted that she wanted something completely different when she envisioned a husband.

But her heart—and her female side—wanted Ty. In fact, her mind and her body were practically enemies at this point, warring with each other, each convinced the other was right.

She'd done a darn good job of moving on, seeking new opportunities. And a new man. Okay, Sam Barr wasn't "the one," but he was the first man she'd gone out with in a long time, and he was nice, and she was looking for *nice* on her man list, wasn't she?

"Go," she told Ty, her voice a little urgent as she gave him a pointed push, practically edging him out of the booth.

He stood, put on his brown Stetson, looked at her a bit sadly with those big brown puppy-dog eyes and tipped his hat to her and Sam before returning to his own booth.

"Poor fellow," Sam said. "Doesn't know what he wants in life."

"Poor fellow?" Jade refused to glance Ty's way. "The man brought you here on a mission. He's not a poor fellow at all. Don't fall for the injured look he wears so well." She sipped water, glad for the coolness, but couldn't meet Sam's eyes.

"He's going to make it," Sam said, his tone admiring. "He's trained for a year to make it through BUD/S. Trained like a maniac. I predict he not only makes it, but he terrorizes all the other recruits."

"Of course he's going to make it!" Jade said, astonished. "All Ty's ever wanted to do was be a SEAL. A lean, mean, fighting machine, as I heard one of the men call him once. He's dedicated to his goal." She swallowed hard. "Ty will make it, and once he does, we'll hardly ever see him around here again." The thought was so painful it physically hurt her stomach.

"Yeah, that's what he told us."

Jade's gaze flew to Sam. "Told you what?"

He shrugged, a handsome lug of good intentions and impeccable character that she felt absolutely no zip, no zing for—not the way Ty kept her emotions all riled up.

"Ty's working on his Plan."

"Plan?"

Sam shrugged. "His life goal. Short list. One, settle some good friends of his—bosom buddies—in BC to tempt the local population of females."

Jade felt her back stiffen. "Go on."

"Two, see his dear friends happily married, with babies, to stifle Robert Donovan's evil plan to turn BC into a concrete wasteland—a project already under way with Donovan in the process of bidding out parcels he owns to various government contractors."

"Let me guess. You and Frog and Squint are the bait for Ty's grand vision."

"And Justin." Sam grinned. "Justin was first, but he took so long to get down to business that Ty began to worry. So he brought the three of us along."

Alarm bells rang inside Jade. "Well, wasn't that thoughtful of Ty. And three?" she asked sweetly.

"Three is to clear his father's name. The murder that was never solved was pinned on his father's incompetence, and that's something Ty also lays at Donovan's door. He's convinced Donovan had a plan to oust his father as sheriff and bankroll the election of his hand-picked pawn of Satan, as Ty puts it." Sam reached for her hand again, going back to the place where they'd been before Ty had butted into their booth.

But they couldn't go back, because once Ty had leaned up against her side, invading her space and her every sense, she'd felt herself slipping. And now that she was hearing of the perfidy of his Plan—who did he think he was, anyway, bringing in men to charm the ladies, as if the BC women were simply a herd of goats—she was really annoyed.

"Fourth, and finally," Sam continued, "the last part of The Plan is for Ty to make it into BUD/S, get his Trident and spend the rest of his days, as long as he can, in every far-flung locale of the world, chasing bad guys. Setting his brothers free." Sam looked thoughtful. "In another life, I do believe Ty would make the perfect assassin. He likes the loner lifestyle. Says he's most at peace when he's alone. Probably because he's adopted, is his theory."

Jade was stunned. She pulled her hand from Sam's, took another sip of her water to calm her racing thoughts.

"That doesn't make sense. Ty was never alone. He was part of our family."

"But that's not how my brother feels. In his mind," Sam said, pointing to his own head. "Ty says he's alone. Got no family, got no one. Says it suits him fine. He was born alone, plans to die alone."

"Is that so." Jade hopped to her feet. "Well, I have something to say to Mr. Loner Spurlock about that. If you'll excuse me, Sam."

Ty Spurlock had another think coming if he thought his Plan was going to work on her. It wasn't—and he wasn't going to zip out of BC under cover of night and leave without her telling his majesty what a nonsensical dumb-ass he was.

This is one lady Ty's going to find it's impossible to bait.

Chapter Two

"Hello, Ty," Jade said, astonishing him because she'd arrived at his booth with something on her mind, judging by the compelling grip she had on his sleeve. "Could I speak to you privately for a moment? Outside?"

Ty glanced at Squint and Frog. "Fellows, I'm being called to duty."

They raised mugs of root beer to Jade. "When duty calls, a gentleman always answers," Frog said.

"If there was a gentleman around," Jade replied, and Ty thought he heard a bit of an edge in the darling little lady's voice. He followed her outside into the bright sunlight, having no choice, really, because she'd let go of him only once he'd left his booth.

Following her was no hardship, since he got to surreptitiously watch that sweet, heart-shaped fanny of hers move ahead of him in a determined locomotion of female-on-a-mission.

Sam must have dropped the ball somehow and upset his conquest. Ty couldn't remember seeing Jade so steamed before, the results of her temper obvious by the lack of a smile on her face and the light frown pulling her brows together. Poor Sam. Nice guy, but a bit too beta male—gentle, sweet, bearlike—for a heart-stopper like Jade.

It was known that women went for the alpha male, the bad boy in boots, which was something Justin Morant, Squint Mathison and sometimes Frog had in abundance. Okay, maybe not Frog; he was pretty beta as beta males went, somehow mellowing after life in the navy. Ty had worried about bringing Sam Barr along for The Plan, fearing he was too easygoing and nice and free-spirited—almost hippielike in his approach to life—then figured maybe BC had a librarian or a kindergarten teacher who might be looking for a plainspoken, existential bear of a man who wouldn't raise her blood pressure.

"Ty Spurlock," Jade said, stopping so fast in the middle of the pavement that he had to reach out and grab her to keep from knocking her down, "who do you think you are?"

He registered soft female and sweet perfume in his arms before he reluctantly released Jade. "What do you mean?"

"I know all about your stupid Plan. And it really is stupid!"

He grinned. "Sam has a big mouth."

"And you have a big head!"

Ty laughed. "Aw, Red. Don't worry." He tugged her back into his arms for a hug disguised as brotherly, but which was just an excuse for him to hold her again. "I didn't leave you out. There are plenty of men to go around." He hesitated, lost for a moment in the scent of peachy shampoo, and the feel of soft curves wriggling against him, before he started to give her a good, brotherly knuckle-rubbing on her scalp. Then his hand suddenly arrested as he realized the knuckle-rub wasn't as satisfying as he'd thought it would be.

Holy crap, she felt good. And sexy as hell.

Jade kicked his ankle, a smart blow he felt even through his jeans and boots. He released her, surprised. "What was that for?"

"You think you're *so* smart."

"Look, Jade. There aren't enough men in this town, you know that. The ladies outnumber us four to one or something. Or ten to one. I'm just trying to do the right thing."

She gazed at him, and he could see disgust heavy in her eyes. "I don't want you doing the right thing for me. Your right thing. Leave me out of The Plan."

He shrugged. "Sweetcake, if you don't like the goods, don't buy them. But it looked like you might like Sam a little bit, from where I was sitting. Pretty cozy lunch the two of you were having."

"So I should fall in with your plan and marry Sam? Is that how this is supposed to work?"

A streak of pain lanced Ty's heart, but just for a moment, and he ignored it for the greater good. "If you fall in love with one of the fine gentlemen I've brought to BC, I would call that a happy ending."

"You're an ass, Ty Spurlock."

He was honestly mystified. "It's no different than a blind date, if you think about it. You've been on a blind date before, haven't you?"

"Yes, but—"

"You'd participate in a bachelorette auction for charity, right? We do those events here every year. The Best Man's Fork run, the Bridesmaids Creek swim—"

"Am I going to the highest bidder?" she asked, and

Ty recognized a warning tone in her voice, which he actually didn't want to hear. He moved quickly to soothe her and ameliorate any damage.

"Now, Jade, as one of Bridesmaids Creek's most generous supporters, you deserve nothing but the best. And I've brought my very best to BC. That being said, if you don't like the fellows, don't go out with them. Sam, Squint and Frog will find other ladies to chat with." Ty tipped his hat, hoped he'd moved off the hot seat, and headed toward his truck with a sigh of relief.

Jade got in the passenger side before he'd even situated himself in the driver's seat. "And what about you? I noticed you left your name off the bachelor offerings."

"I'm not eligible." He started his truck, backing up. "If you're riding with me, buckle up. If not, advise me where I may drop you off. You wouldn't want to keep Sam waiting, I would presume."

She gave him a decidedly annoyed eyeing. "You really are a jackass, aren't you?"

"So they say. You coming?"

Jade leaned back, buckled her seat belt. "I'm not done telling you off."

"Fine by me. We ride together, but you may not like the destination." He glanced at her, ridiculously happy to have Jade in his truck—and happy as hell that she wasn't back at The Wedding Diner being romanced by Sam.

Which was kind of bad, because Sam had only been doing what he'd come to BC to do: find a wife. Or at least that's what Ty had told Sam and the guys they wanted: a wife, and a chance to have a family, become dads. Ty had promised them that BC was ripe, full-to-bursting ripe, with ladies who would leap at the chance to run to the altar.

He sighed. "So what's the topic?"

"Topic?"

He looked at her long, slim legs in Wranglers, the dangerous look in her eyes. Curves in all the right places. Was pretty certain his libido was starting to smoke. "The topic you're in my truck to discuss."

"Let's start with your Plan."

"Everybody has to have one, little lady. Otherwise nothing ever gets done." He rolled down his window, happy to smell fresh country air, be driving a truck in the greatest little town on earth, and have the most dynamite sexy redhead he knew glaring at him from the safety of her seat belt. "You have a problem with plans?"

"*The* Plan. The Plan that seems to start with you bringing bachelors to town, getting them married, and then you skittering off like a cockroach."

"I see no problem with that plan. Sounds like all the holes are filled." He frowned. "Maybe a slight quibble with the cockroach part. Don't think I ever saw myself in that role." Ty brightened. "You could rephrase it as Ty rides off into the sunset, leaving behind a grateful town. A veritable hero, and the townspeople cheered their thanks."

"Ass," she murmured under her breath.

"*Hero.*"

"Okay, but say someone decides you're the catch of the day before you go—"

"Riding off like a *hero*."

"Skittering off like—"

"It is understood by all," he interrupted quickly, before she could bring up the roach bit again, because in the mood she apparently was in, she was going to get around to saying something about how roaches got squished under female boots, "that I've never been a marrying man. This has never even been questioned."

"Ah, the happy, footloose, untamed cowboy."

"Exactly," he said, pleased now that they understood each other perfectly.

"Which is why you interrupted my lunch with Sam."

"Why?"

"Because you don't think Sam's the man for me. Obviously."

"Well," Ty said, uncomfortably acknowledging that what she'd said held the ring of truth, "there are better options."

"And who would those better options be? Because quite frankly, Sam suits me."

"How?"

"He's nice. He's gentle. He says what he means. Unlike some people, who are full of baloney."

Ty supposed she meant him. She certainly had that you're-the-guy-full-of-baloney tone in her voice. "I take it you're not happy I interrupted your lunch."

"Face it, Ty, you've always been something of a showboat."

"You mean I live life large." He sneaked another glance at her shapely body, red-hot from the flaming topknot of hair to her boots. "I remember when you and I used to play with our friends all day in the fields. Ball, chase, Red Rover—if it was a game, we knew it." He sighed. "I miss those days sometimes." He didn't understand how his best friend had grown up to be such a siren. Jade had him tied in knots he wasn't sure could be undone, except maybe by some kind of spell. Or his absence. "I'll be leaving soon," he said, reaching for the easiest knot to untie.

"Good," she said pleasantly.

His lips twisted of their own accord. "Guess that means no going-away party." Or kiss, for that matter.

"I wish you the best of luck. I hope you make it through BUD/S. You've worked hard enough to get there."

He turned his head at the soft, earnest note to her voice, surprised. "I believe you mean that."

"With all my heart." She opened the door when he stopped at the last crosshatch of road at the town's edge. "See you around, Ty."

"You can't get out here." They were a good two miles from the main drag. He didn't want her to leave, anyway. He'd been enjoying having her in his truck, even though he sensed she had something urgent on her mind.

"I'll be fine. Sam followed us."

She waved, closed the door, and as she headed to the truck behind his, which was indeed Sam Barr's vehicle, Ty's last glimpse of Jade was her sweet fanny as she got on the running board and scooted up into the passenger seat. He blinked, stunned by how fast he'd lost her. Damn Sam for being such a resourceful fellow, Ty thought, recognizing at the same time that Sam had many fine qualities, resourcefulness notwithstanding, or Ty would never have brought him here as an outstanding, trustworthy candidate to be won by the ladies of BC.

But he didn't have to be *so* darn resourceful.

"It was like taking candy from a baby," Sam observed to his two friends as they perched in the bunkhouse at the Hanging H ranch. Their friend—and project—Justin Morant had married Mackenzie Hawthorne here not so many months ago, making himself the proud father of four little girls. Justin had kept the three amigos—as he called Squint, Sam and Frog—on at the Hanging H, saying he had big plans to expand the spread and operations. They would also need a lot of help when they put the Haunted H into full swing, the renaissance of Bridesmaids Creek's beloved "haunted" house and amusement place for kiddies and families. This October, they'd be putting the haunted back in the Hanging H, and BC was buzzing with the return of one of their most profitable and renowned projects.

"Candy from a baby?" Squint said. "Even a baby has better sense than Ty."

Frog grinned. "I figure putting you up to following Ty around was a stroke of genius. There you were, the proverbial white knight, when Jade decided she needed a ride away from temptation."

Sam sank into the leather sectional sofa in the comfortable bunkhouse, sighing with pleasure. "They say a man doesn't know what he's lost until it's gone. And the only way to capture Ty in his own snare is to make him think the bait is about to be stolen."

They all crowed about that, lifting beer bottles to each other in victory.

"What we need is a real challenge," Frog said.

The room went silent.

"I don't believe there's anything more challenging than getting Ty Spurlock to pull his head out of his butt," Sam offered. "What do you have in mind?"

"Well, let's see." Frog gazed at the ceiling. "The haunted house will start by the end of this month, for nine glorious months of family fun. Then BC kicks off Christmas Wonderland all over town, and Santa Claus takes over right after Thanksgiving. What do you say,"

Frog said, warming to his idea, "if we give ourselves a two-week deadline to get Ty and Jade engaged?"

Squint looked at him doubtfully. "What you're really aiming for is to get Ty off the dime before he leaves for BUD/S. That's just not going to happen. You know as well as anyone, since you were by my side in Afghanistan, that a BUD/S candidate is encouraged to take care of any detail that might be a distraction before he gets to training. Along that topic, a candidate is also discouraged from taking on new decisions, such as a wife. I say hold your horses, there, son. BUD/S is serious stuff."

"Then why are we doing this? Why are we trying to pull the rug out from under Ty?" Sam shook his head. "It'd be unfair to Jade if we're all going to wave goodbye to Ty in a couple of weeks, and her heart is broken."

"That's why an engagement is even more important." Frog nodded wisely. "No questions left unanswered."

"There are too many questions," Squint said direly. "You forget there was a murder here years ago that was never solved. Ty hasn't forgotten that the lack of an arrest was put down to his father's bungling of the investigation. He's not going to pop any questions until his dad's name is cleared. And the only way to clear it is to reopen the Haunted H, and let everyone see that the past is the past. Whatever happened then no longer matters."

They considered that.

"I guess so," Sam said. "We're not being fair to Jade, then. She doesn't want a man who's all hung up in his head."

"No," Frog agreed. "She'd be better off with you."

"Yeah, but I don't want to settle down," Sam declared. "I want to see Ty caught in his own trap!"

"Then we'll have to work around the murder angle,"

Squint said, "Frog and I'll focus on Daisy Donovan, since it was her old man who was determined to destroy the Haunted Hanging H and brought this whole house of cards down on Ty. And you try to wrangle Ty to the altar, preferably before he ships out."

"Great," Sam said. "You took the easy assignment, and left me to corral the man who brought us here to find brides for ourselves."

"Thought you just said you don't want a bride," Squint pointed out.

"It's true," Sam said, downcast. "I just came along for the ride, and to see the two of you suffer. Then you decided to make Ty suffer, and that seemed like even more fun. But it's not so much fun anymore," he groused.

"It'll be worth it when we see Ty heading up the altar path," Frog said, exhorting his friends to action. "Shake on it, fellows. We've got a lot of work to do."

TY WAS SO annoyed with his friends and a certain sexy redhead that when Daisy Donovan slid up under his arm in the parking lot of the sheriff's office, all he could do was muster up an unenthusiastic, "Hi, Daze."

She gave him a friendly enough squeeze, but where Donovans were concerned, it was like being in a boa constrictor's grip—you knew it wasn't going to end well unless you could get away fast.

The tempestuous brunette bombshell had no inclination to remove herself from his side. "So much man, Ty Spurlock, and somehow, all I ever feel for you is sisterly emotions."

"That's what they tell me. What's on your mind?"

She laughed, hot allure practically snapping sparks his way—which meant Daisy wanted something.

"You."

"I'm not available." His gaze lit on Jade heading into Madame Matchmaker's comfortable, cheery, pink-fronted shop, and his stomach bottomed out. What could Jade possibly want with Madame Lafleur?

No doubt it was just a simple visit. Madame Matchmaker and Mssr. Unmatchmaker—Cosette and Phillipe Lafleur—had offices right next to each other, connected internally by an arched door that could be locked for privacy when they had clients. Phillipe and Cosette had been married for fifty years, bickered constantly, loved each other like mad and had recently decided they were going to unmake their own marriage. This decision had BC residents in a twist, not certain whether the matchmaking/unmatchmaking services still had good karma. Cosette kept a book of all the matches she'd put together—and of the "mismatches," only one was recorded in her book: that of Mackenzie Hawthorne's marriage to Tommy Fields. Tommy had left Mackenzie for a twenty-year-old, and since Ty had been responsible for bringing Tommy to Cosette's attention to make the match, he'd felt compelled to bring a replacement to BC for Mackenzie: Justin Morant.

It was a match made in heaven. But since Ty knew that Cosette's matches didn't always go off as planned, he worried about Jade slipping into the pink shop with the scrolled lettering on the window that read Madame Matchmaker Premiere Matchmaking Service. Where Love Comes True.

He didn't want love coming true for Jade, at least not with anyone but himself.

"I really am a rat bastard," he murmured, and Daisy said, "What?"

"Nothing." He looked down at the brunette attached to his arm. "Did you say you needed something, Daisy? I have to be somewhere."

"I want you. Remember?" She smiled at him, a veritable temptress with something on her mind.

Stepped right into that, and now he was almost afraid to ask. "You just said you have sisterly emotions for me. Can you be more specific about this 'want'?"

She glanced at the jail, which was buried deep inside the courthouse, just the way Sheriff Dennis liked it. "Going to see the sheriff about something?"

He'd forgotten all about seeing Sheriff Dennis once he'd spotted Jade. It almost didn't bear thinking about what pink-haired Cosette and his sassy redheaded darling might be dreaming up between them.

It certainly didn't bear thinking that Jade might be chatting with Cosette concerning Sam. *Sam, my friend, who I brought here,* Ty reminded himself. "Nothing set in stone."

"Good. Because I have a problem. And I need your big, strong muscles and wise mind to help me."

She beamed up at him, daddy's little girl, who'd never heard the word *no* in her life. Ty cleared his throat.

"What, Daisy?" He couldn't wait to get away and make an unscheduled visit to Phillipe, see if he could figure out what was going on behind the arched doorway of the two shops. Maybe the door would be open, and he could listen to what Cosette and Jade had up their dainty sleeves.

"I need a man," Daisy said. "And you'll do just fine."

Chapter Three

"What are they doing?" Jade asked, peering through the white slats at the window of Cosette's private sanctum. She couldn't see Daisy and Ty; Cosette had a much better vantage point. "If I know Daisy, she'll be kissing Ty before he even knows it's happening."

"I don't have a great view." Cosette strained her femininely plump body a little harder to peer out. "But it looks like Daisy's plastered all over him. She wants something."

Jade backed away from the window, telling herself it didn't matter. She shouldn't care. She plopped into a pink velvet antique chair and waited for Cosette to give her a further bulletin.

"Ah, there goes the kiss," Cosette said. "I knew Daisy would hit her mark."

Jade shot out of her chair, mashing the slats flat in her hurry to see what she really didn't want to see. But all she saw was Ty striding away from Daisy, who watched him from in front of the small courthouse as he crossed the street. Jade snapped the blinds shut before he could catch her spying.

"Gotcha!" Cosette laughed delightedly, taking the pink chair opposite as Jade returned to hers.

Jade stared at her friend. "You mean Ty and Daisy weren't kissing?"

Cosette looked coy. "Of course not. That would never happen. But what do you care?"

"I don't." She did. Terribly.

"My girl, it's no use protesting. That's no way to catch a man. It's very American to be hard to get, and with some men that works. However, Ty's leaving soon. You don't have time to set traps."

Jade wrinkled her nose. "Let's talk about why I've come to see you." It would be best to get Cosette off the topic of trapping Ty. She had no idea how badly the man annoyed Jade.

It annoyed her even more that Cosette could tell that she did care if Ty kissed Daisy, or anyone.

"You can talk about whatever you like," Cosette said pleasantly. "In your mind, you'll still be thinking about Ty."

Jade drew a deep breath, telling herself to be patient with her older friend. "I assure you, I'm not thinking of Ty."

"Did I hear my name?" Ty appeared in the arched doorway, broad-shouldered and fine, and Jade's breath caught in spite of her wishing it wouldn't.

"Why would we be talking about you?" she asked, giving Cosette the don't-say-a-word eyeball.

"Why wouldn't you be?" He walked in and lounged on the prim white sofa across from their pink tufted chairs, eyed the delicate teacups on the table, ready for tea, and the pink-and-white petits fours invitingly arranged on a silver tray. "I saw you two spies. You're leading Jade down a bad path, Madame." He laughed, pleased with himself, a big moose with way too much confidence.

Jade scowled. "Everybody spies on Daisy."

"Of course we were spying on you!" Cosette said. "Jade had just told me how very handsome you looked today." She smiled hugely. "You don't mind if we ladies checked you out, do you, Ty?" Cosette rose with a distinctly coquettish air. "If you will both excuse me for a moment, I think I hear Phillipe calling my name. No doubt he's sniffed the aroma of petits fours and tea all the way from his dusty office. The man adores my petits fours." She swept out of the room, a vision in pink, white and silver, a lady on a mission.

Jade turned back to find Ty's gaze on her, his eyes squinting with internal smirk-itude. "Oh, don't go getting a big head over Cosette's comments."

"Where there's smoke, there's fire. Do please pour." He nodded toward the teacups.

"There was no smoke, no fire. We weren't looking at you." Jade leaned over to pour out the tea, then handed him a cup. "You can get your own petit four if you want it."

He laughed. "I do, in fact, want to try Phillipe's favorite treat. What is it about these tiny things you ladies find so irresistible?"

She hoped to get him off the topic of his handsomeness—which she had said nothing about to Cosette, though she had, in fact, been thinking that he was extraordinarily hunky—and the topic of tiny frosted cakes was as safe as any. "It's the art involved in a petit four."

"So in other words, you really don't want me to bring up that Cosette gave you away?" He winked, bit into a cake. "Whatever you want, doll."

Jade sent him a sour look. "What did Daisy want?"

"This is good," Ty said, his tone surprised. "Sugary, sweet, delicate. Couldn't eat a lot, far too rich for that, but tasty all the same. If you eat too many of these, you'll have to watch that sexy figure of yours."

"Back to Daisy. Quit avoiding the fact that you were conversing with the enemy."

"Oh, that." He put his plate down, picked up his tea and sipped. It looked quite ridiculous, she thought, a big man holding a fragile cup and saucer—and yet, somehow, she wanted so badly to kiss him she didn't know what to do.

Which was such a bad thought to have she wished it right out of her brain. "Yes, that. I'm going to bug you until you tell, so get on with it."

"Nothing important. And on that note, I should depart—"

"I'll ask Daisy myself, and whatever she wanted, she'll embellish," Jade warned.

"She wants me to escort her to the grand opening of the Haunted H," Ty said, his tone reluctant, his expression even more so.

Jade blinked. "But why? She and her father got up a petition to keep the Haunted H from starting again. They were violently opposed, and part of the reason we waited was to make sure folks in Bridesmaids Creek supported it."

"Daisy says it'll show everyone that bygones are bygones. She doesn't want to go by herself, and being escorted by—"

"By the man who brought the bachelors to Bridesmaids Creek will make her look like the belle of the ball," Jade interrupted.

Ty seemed confused. "I don't think that was what she's after. Granted, Daisy's no innocent flower, but she really sounded sincere."

Jade raised a brow. "Really, really sincere. Daisy, sincere." Surely that wasn't jealousy in her tone. But then she realized by the reappearance of his smirk that he was thinking the same thing.

"You know you're a special girl, Jade," he began.

She hopped to her feet. "Ty, you bigheaded oaf, don't you take that tone with me. I don't care if you go with Daisy. I just think you're a traitor. It's not fair to Mackenzie and Justin, because Daisy's done everything she can to destroy the Hanging H getting its haunting back. You *know* that."

"Yeah." Ty sounded momentarily confused again. "You have a point."

"And you know what Daisy's father said about your own father," Jade stated, warming to her subject, wanting badly for Ty to see for himself that he'd fallen prey to Daisy's charms, as every man in BC seemed to do eventually. "Robert Donovan said your father bungled the investigation of the murder out at the Hanging H—"

"Daisy said us going to the opening together would let everyone know that those days were past," Ty said. "I really thought it was in the Haunted H's—and Bridesmaids Creek's—best interests that I escort her. I'm leaving in less than two weeks. What I want more than anything is to leave behind a town with a secure future, with everyone on the same page."

He looked distressed. Jade felt sorry for him, so sorry her heart hurt. Maybe she was beating him up because she was jealous. *I am jealous,* she admitted to herself.

But nothing good ever came of associating with Daisy Donovan and her land-grabbing father. "I've got to go."

"Hang on a sec—" Ty said, but Jade couldn't stay any longer. She hated all of it—hated that Ty was leaving most of all. What if she never saw him again?

She hurried out the door and jumped into her truck, vaguely aware that Daisy stood on the pavement outside Madame Matchmaker's shop, smiling her infamous bad-girl smile.

TY WAS THUNDERSTRUCK, and could not have been more shell-shocked, when Jade left in a hurry. He'd been this close to her—in the same room, and kindly left alone by Madame Matchmaker—and he'd blown it. Big mouth, big feet into big mouth, bad combo.

"Crap," he said, when Cosette hurried back into the room, her eyes distressed and her pink-tinted hair slightly mussed from her rush. "I think I just blew that."

"Oh, dear." She handed him a small plate of homemade lasagna, steam rising from the cheesy top. "Eat for strength. Eat for intuition."

He looked at the lasagna, a four-by-four piece he would have devoured under any other circumstances, say, had Jade not ditched him, leaving him with a guilty conscience and a terrible case of buyer's remorse where Daisy was concerned. "Will it help?"

"Oh, lasagna always helps," Cosette assured him. "A big man like yourself doesn't do well on an empty stomach."

He thought that sounded like the first sane advice he'd had all day, and dug in with the silver fork she'd put on his plate.

He actually felt a little stronger, and perhaps a bit of

clarity come over him—it was too soon for intuition—
as the warm food hit his stomach. "I'm in the doghouse
with Jade."

"Yes." Cosette nodded. "Probably so."

"Trying to do the right thing isn't always easy."

"Indeed it's not. But doing a dumb thing is very easy."

He gazed at her. "Were you just subtly trying to prod
me into self-discovery mode?"

"Not so wordy, dear. Just trying to help you pull your
head out of your keister, as you young folks put it."

"Ah." He ate some more lasagna. "Does Jade like
me?"

"A little," Cosette said. "You did spend a lot of time
being raised by her mother, if you recall. She got used
to you."

"Yeah. Jade was an awesome little sister." Only he
hadn't felt sisterly toward her in a long, long time.

"Things change," Cosette observed.

"Daisy might have changed."

"And some things don't ever change."

Ty nodded. "You think there's no way to leave the
past behind and move on with our lives? The Donovans
can't mean it when they say they want to be part of BC?"

"Some things are just habit." Cosette shrugged. "No,
I don't think the Donovans are being any more forth-
right than they've ever been."

Why was he training to be a SEAL if he didn't believe in the greater good? "Eventually this town has to
move on."

"I'm impressed that you want to forgive the Donovans, given how your father was treated by them when
he was sheriff."

Ty's blood hit low boil, began to simmer at the old,

painful memories. He put his plate on the marble-topped coffee table. "I'm just trying to leave town on a good note. I want there to be healing, Cosette. No divisions in the town on my behalf."

"Are you not planning on coming back, then? Because this town wrote the book on divisions. We feel pretty safe with black and white, good and evil. We're not trying to be a storybook town, Ty. We sell our charms and our legends, always with a hefty dose of fairy tale evil villains."

He looked at her. "You and Phillipe aren't really getting a divorce, are you?"

She stared at him. "Young man, how is that any of your business? I suspect you have plenty of your own love life to attend to."

He got up from the chair. "You never did say whether you believe Jade feels more than sisterly to me."

"But we've already established your head is firmly lodged in your hindquarters, dear, so what good would it do for me to try to help you with the answer?" Cosette walked him to the door. "I have no words of wisdom for you."

"No words of guidance from the local matchmaker?" He was teasing, but only slightly. He really wanted to know how Jade felt, because he was definitely getting some kind of strange vibe from her.

"A little bit of guidance, just a smidge, if you're in the mood to hear it," the matchmaker said. "Jade needs to be able to trust a man. Completely."

Cosette closed the door behind him.

Great. Jade didn't seem to trust him much.

Right now, Ty really didn't trust himself.

SUZ HAWTHORNE, MACKENZIE'S little sister and part-owner of the Hanging H ranch, launched herself at Ty the moment he returned to the bunkhouse. "Are you an idiot?" she demanded. "A certifiable idiot?"

Ty slumped into the leather recliner, noting that Sam, Squint and Frog were all there to witness his takedown. "Probably. On which topic are we speaking?"

The thing about Suz was that she instantly commanded respect—if a fellow wanted to keep his hat attached to his head. Twenty-three and spunky, recently retired from the Peace Corps, she had come home to help her sister save the Hanging H, preserving it for herself and Mackenzie, but mostly for Mackenzie's four newborns. You only had to look at Suz to realize she probably could make your life miserable if she cared to, Ty realized. He eyed her short spiky hair, streaked blue over blond, and the cheek stud that complemented her dark eyes—eyes that glared at him even as he stared back at her.

"Kissing Daisy?" Suz demanded. "You're not a certifiable idiot. You're a certifiable dumb-ass!"

"I did not kiss Daisy."

Suz's glare went DEFCON on him. "The grapevine says differently. You of all people know Daisy Donovan is poison to us!"

His brothers-in-mischief looked at him with great sympathy.

"She has a point, bro," Frog said.

"Poison or not, Daisy's *hot,*" Squint said, earning himself astonished stares from everyone.

Sam grinned. "Doesn't mean she'd be good for you."

"You can talk, Sam," Ty said. "You're just going to ride away one day. This is my town. I have to stay on everyone's good side because eventually I'll be pushing up daisies here with the rest of my fellow residents, and I don't expect to get any more peace in the afterlife than I've gotten in BC in the present life. Staying on everybody's good side is an art form." And right now, he wasn't on Suz's good side. "Look, little sister—"

"Don't 'little sister' me." Even with the wild hair, the piercings and the discreet tats, Suz was beautiful in her own way—and her expressive eyes right now stabbed him with guilt. "Daisy and her father tried to kill off the haunted house before it ever got started. If you're so interested in saving Bridesmaids Creek, you'll know that you can't show up with the enemy. Or be sucking face with her, either."

Suz shot the men a last look of disgust and departed. Ty's friends checked him for his reaction.

"She has a point," Squint said. "I'll save you. I'll suck face with Daisy."

"She's a fireball. Won't ever glance your way unless there's something she wants from you." Ty looked at his boots, which he'd propped on the coffee table, in direct violation of the house rules he had engraved on his mind from years of living under Jade and Betty's roof. "In fact, I think I got snookered."

"What were you thinking?" Frog peered out the window after Suz. "That is some fine little lady, by the way."

"And that's not going to happen, either." Ty got to his feet. "Not at the pace you three are moving." He felt distinctly glum about his dilemma. "Do you knuckleheads understand I'm leaving town soon? I won't be here to guide the reins of romance for you."

Sam laughed. "There's no such thing, bro. Romance

isn't guided. It's a whirlwind of passion, joy, misunderstanding and longing."

They all gazed at Sam, who shrugged.

"I'm just saying," he told them. "If you really want romance, you have to let the whirlwind suck you into its vortex."

"I've had enough of sucking faces and whirlwind vortexes. One of you is going to have to escort Daisy to the opening. You must go in my stead, as my representative. It'll be a poor substitute," Ty said grandly, "but a man doesn't go back on his promise." He pulled a quarter from his pocket. "Here's how we'll decide which of you will—"

"Lash himself to the mast of misfortune," Frog butted in. "None of us wants to be saddled with the mistress of mayhem."

"You're all so poetic today. This is how this works." Ty put the quarter on the top of his fist. "Each of you will call heads or tails. The one who calls wrong wins the prize."

"Some prize," Sam said. "I don't see why we should have to clean up your mess, dude."

"Because I brought you here."

"In other words, no gain without pain. I call heads," Sam said.

"Is it a two-headed coin?" Squint asked. "It'd be like you to have a two-headed coin."

Ty gawked at his friend's lack of trust in him. "Would a SEAL candidate scam his best buddies?"

"I'll call heads, too," Frog sighed.

"I'll take tails," Squint said, "just to liven things up."

Ty tossed the coin, let it land on the Southwestern-style loomed rug. The quarter stared at them.

"That's it, then," Squint said, "I'm your fall guy."

Frog and Sam leaned back on the leather sofas, oozing relief. Ty picked up his quarter.

"I thought you said you wanted to kiss Daisy," Ty said to Squint.

"I thought I did. I think I just got really cold feet." He looked suddenly apprehensive. "It was one thing to have the fantasy. It's another to have the fantasy sprung on you in all its—"

"Soft, delicate flesh." Sam hopped up, clapped Ty on the shoulder. "Thanks for the good flip. I'm off to hunt up trouble at the big house."

"Big house?" Ty watched Frog shoot to his feet, following Sam to the door. "You mean the Hanging H? Are you going to see Suz?"

"I am," Sam said. "Frog's not." He glared at his buddy. "You stay here with them. I don't need any deadweight."

Frog hurried out the door in front of Sam, in a rush to get to Suz first. Sam glanced back at Squint and Ty with a grin. "He's so easy to work. A little spark of jealousy and watch those boots fly."

He closed the door. Ty sighed. "Thanks for taking Daisy on for me. I just can't afford any drama right now. Not when I'm leaving." He sank into the sofa. Of course, his relief had nothing to do with his departure; it was all about Jade. Once he'd realized he had stepped in a huge pile of cosmic poo, he knew he had to back out on Daisy no matter what it took. There was no way he wanted Jade upset with him.

"You're crazy about that little lady, aren't you?"

Of course he wasn't crazy about Jade. What a dumb thing to say. "Don't try to make romance bloom in a desert, Squint."

Jade blew in on a flurry of cold wind and a gust of snow that slithered from the bunkhouse roof. Ty straightened, stunned that she was here, glad as heck to see her.

"I think I'll join the fellows and see what trouble we can conjure up," Squint said, disappearing.

Some friend, taking off when it was clear there was going to be a sonic boom leveled at him. Ty looked at Jade, appreciating the tall redhead's sass as she put her hands on her slender hips and gazed at him with disgust.

"Daisy Donovan," she said.

"I felt sorry for her."

"You did not." Jade glared at him. "Daisy tried to ruin my business. She's trying to ruin the Hawthornes' haunted house, which, may I remind you, is something that could bring Bridesmaids Creek back to life. As I recall, that was your stated purpose in returning with three bachelors, wasn't it? New blood to breathe new life into the moribund shell that is Bridesmaids Creek?"

He loved looking at this woman. He loved hearing her talk, even when she was railing at him. When she said words like *moribund,* her lips pursed so cutely it was all he could do not to jump up and take those lips with his mouth, hungrily diving into the sweet sex appeal that was Jade.

Hell, he wasn't 100 percent certain what *moribund* meant—although it sounded distinctly dire—but maybe if he let her talk long enough, she'd say something else that started with *m-o-r.* He decided not to confess that he'd already dumped Daisy off on Squint, and to let the little lady fuss at him.

"Don't you have anything to say for yourself?" Jade demanded.

"I'm content to let you do all the talking." He settled himself comfortably, watching her face. "You have something on your mind, and I'm happy to let you clear the deck."

She sat next to him, so she could look closely at him to press her case, he supposed. But the shock of having her so near to him—almost in his space—was enough to brain-wipe what little sense he had. Damn, she smelled good, like spring flowers breaking through a long, cold winter. He shook his head to clear the sudden madness diluting his gray matter. "You're beautiful," he said, the words popping out before he could put on the Dumb-ass Brake.

The Dumb-ass Brake had saved him many a time, but today, it seemed to have gotten stuck.

"What?" Jade said. Her mesmerizing green eyes stared at him, stunned.

He was half drowning, might as well go for full immersion. "You're beautiful," he repeated.

She looked at him for a long moment, then scoffed. "Ty Spurlock, don't you dare try to sweet-talk me. If there's one thing I know about you, it's that sugar flows out of your mouth like a river of honey when you're making a mess. The bigger the jam, the sweeter and deeper the talk." She got up, putting several feet of safety between them, and Ty cursed the disappearance of the brake that had deserted him just when he'd needed it most.

"Okay, so if sweet talk won't save me," he said, reverting to cavalier, since that's what she seemed to be expecting, "all I can say is that Daisy asked me to take her to the grand opening, and you didn't."

"I didn't want to ask you!"

"Then why are we having this conversation? Good

old-fashioned green-eyed monster, maybe?" He got up, took her in his arms. "I'll talk sweet to you if you want me to, beautiful."

She stomped on his toe and moved out of his arms. He bent over, his toe impressed by the sudden squelching it had cruelly received.

"What I want you to do is tell Daisy Donovan you wouldn't be caught dead escorting her to the haunted house. No smart remarks about puns." Jade glared at him. "And from now on, I suggest you remember who your real friends are."

He fell onto the sofa, wondering if she'd broken his toe. Definitely he was going to donate a toenail to the cause. Not a good thing to have happen right before he left for BUD/S. "I know who my friends are. They're the ones who don't try to damage me right before I leave for SEAL training."

"I don't care about that," Jade said sweetly. "I care that you don't fall into one of Daisy's many traps, and leave drama back here in BC for me to clean up. You're just lucky I got to you before Suz did."

"She's already been here. Only she didn't wound me." Ty glanced at his secret sweetie's boots with respect. Square-toed and sturdy, they could have been registered weapons.

"She didn't? Maybe she's going soft. But I'm not. I know who my friends are." Jade walked over, tugged his boot off. "I also know how commerce works in this town, and I understand Daisy's tricky little mind. Oh, you big baby," she said, staring at the toe she'd rescued from his boot and sock. "It's just going to be a little black-and-blue. You'd better toughen up if you're going to make it through training."

He smelled that sweet perfume again, was riveted by the soft red sweater covering her delicate breasts. Wondered if playing the pitiful card would get him attached to her lips—and decided he probably didn't want to do anything to upset the grudging sympathy he finally saw in her eyes. "My toe is fine. My life is fine. Everything is fine."

"It's not fine yet." She smiled, leaned over and gave him a long, sweet, not-sisterly-at-all smooch on the lips. Shocked, he sat as still as a concrete gargoyle, frozen and immobilized, too scared to move and frighten her off.

She pulled away far too soon. "*Now* it's fine."

Indeed it was. He couldn't stop staring at her mouth, which had worked such magic on him, stolen his breath, stolen his heart. He gazed into her eyes, completely lost in the script.

"What was that for?"

Jade got up, went to the door, opening it. Cold air rushed in and a supersized sheet of snow fell from the overhang, but he couldn't take his eyes off her.

"Because I felt like it," Jade said, then left.

Damn. His toe still throbbed, but his lips were practically sizzling from her kiss, far outweighing the complaining from his phalange bone. Ty had no idea what the hell had just happened here—but it dawned on him through his shell-shocked, sex-driven, Jade-desiring brain that if he were a smart man, he'd better decline Daisy's invitation on the double, let her know he was sending a stand-in.

If he ever wanted to be kissed like that again.

Chapter Four

The night of the grand opening of the refurbished, re-born Haunted H was glorious, by anyone's standards. Ty felt a real sense of satisfaction as he looked at the new lights his buddies had put up in an elegant arch over the long drive-up to the ranch. Lights were everywhere, twinkling and beautiful, highlighting the butt-freezing weather and somehow making it romantic.

Maybe his three bachelor candidates weren't totally useless, after all. They could at least decorate, apparently, if not appropriately seduce the women he'd brought them here to romance.

Ty hurried after Jade when he saw her moving with long strides toward the jump house, which was teeming with kiddies. Parents with strollers watched, smiling, as their kids bounced inside the huge, inflatable pink-and-purple castle.

"Hi, Raggedy Ann," he said, and Jade turned to look at him. He thought she was amazing with her red curls springing out everywhere, completely negating the need for a Raggedy Ann wig. The red-and-white stockings were killer, clinging to dynamite legs Raggedy Ann never dreamed of having in her cloth-stuffed world. He nearly had a coronary over the cute painted freckles speckled across Jade's nose and cheeks, never mind the white apron over the blue dress, which for some reason made him very horny. He supposed the truth was that everything about Jade caught him between a coronary and an erection, a delicious in-between hell of longing and teeth-grinding lust.

She gave him a once-over. "What are you dressed up as?"

He was pretty proud of his efforts, and drew himself up to showcase the black cape, boots and swashbuckling ebony hat he thought he wore so stylishly. "Zorro. You couldn't tell?"

"You look silly." She offered him the tray she held. "Cupcake?"

"What do you mean, I look silly?" Ty demanded. "Ladies love Zorro. They think he's a dashing hero. And sexy."

"Guy Williams was sexy. Antonio Banderas was a sexy Zorro." She gave Ty another once-over. "Please take a cupcake so I'll feel better about deflating your monstrous ego."

Ty ignored the cupcake, wishing he could have a kiss instead. "Where did I go wrong?"

"I don't have time to tell you all the ways that costume is wrong." She laughed and started to move away. "Where's your date?"

Ah. The little lady was prickly because she was expecting Daisy to land on his arm any moment. He felt better now that he knew her lack of charmed respect for his costume was thanks to jealousy. "Squint's escorting her."

Jade moved away. "By now you have to wonder where you're going wrong, Ty. When Daisy Donovan throws you over, and you only put on half your mustache, something's not working for you."

She disappeared into the crowd. He felt his upper lip. Frog and Sam banged him on the back. Ty coughed, thinking he could easily survive BUD/S, since he could survive the camaraderie of his so-called friends in BC. "Easy on the lungs and rib cage, fellows."

"Where's your 'stache?" Frog demanded.

Ty looked at Frog, dressed as a fairly convincing Robin Hood, and Sam, who was masquerading as a pirate. Both of them had their mustaches firmly in place. Ty felt around in his pocket for the left side of his. "Thought I had it on."

They smirked. "Smart-asses," he said, realizing his friends had let him walk out of the bunkhouse missing half his facial prop. "Friends don't let friends go out missing the most important part of their costume. The mustache is the sex-magnet angle for Zorro."

They seemed to think that was hilarious. "Look," Frog said, "Sam snapped a photo when you weren't looking. It's pretty much gone viral on the internet."

The photo showed Ty trying to get his hat just right in the mirror, really working hard for Zorro-mysterious, completely missing the fact that one side of his upper lip was traumatically bare. "You guys are such a riot."

"Yeah." Frog wiped tears of laughter from his eyes and put his phone away. "That we are."

"So, was Jade bowled over by your sex appeal?" Sam asked, loudly enough that half the county could hear the question, even over the whirring of air keeping the bounce house inflated, and the squeals from delighted kids.

"Not really," Ty admitted. "She seemed to be under

the impression that I was here with Daisy. Every piece of gossip transmits itself at warp speed in BC, but for some reason not the one bit of info that really mattered reached her ears." He glared at his buddies. "You two are useless."

"You gotta talk your own book, brother," Frog said. "We can't do all your heavy lifting for you."

"Yeah, don't expect us to sell the steak if it ain't sizzling on its own," Sam said, and they drifted off, vastly amused with themselves.

Ty sighed and went to man the dunk booth as he'd promised Jade's mother, Betty, that he would.

"Don't you look hot," Daisy said at his elbow. She was dressed like a princess, of course. What else would anyone have expected? "Hot as a pistol!"

Ty perked up at the rather corny appreciation of his efforts. "Thanks."

"No problem." She traced his upper lip where there should have been a sweet Zorro-inspired clump of faux bristles. "I have my face paints with me, since I'm in charge of face painting. I can fix that in a jiff."

He was pretty relieved to hear it, even though he was surprised Daisy had been given any assignment at all, up until the point she began slowly, sensually painting on his upper lip with a brush. A crowd gathered around the princess and Zorro, and he wondered desperately where Squint was.

Ty could have predicted with the accuracy of seven oracles that Jade would catch him with his chin firmly clutched in Daisy's, well, clutches, her face inches from his.

"Well, at least it's a mustache now," Jade said, "instead of half a confused black caterpillar."

"I think he looks sexy as hell," Daisy said, and planted one right on his cheek. Ty's eyes went wide. His body recognized hot sex appeal and his inner guide reacted urgently, screaming *Fire! Fire! Danger!*

He leaped away from Daisy, just in time to see Jade heading off toward the ice cream booth her mother ran, a very popular spot surrounded by anxious kids wanting sprinkles on their ice cream and parents wanting hot chocolate.

"I heard a rumor," Daisy said, "that Jade Harper made you dump me tonight."

"Ah…" Ty tried to glimpse Raggedy Ann's hot red curls in the crowd near the ice-cream stand. "She didn't approve," he said, his brain belatedly registering that he probably should have censored that remark.

"I see," Daisy said. She leaned up against his chest. "You don't know what you're missing."

He stared down at the determined, dynamite bundle of feminine firepower his buddy Squint seemed to think he could handle. *Hell, no, Squint can't handle this. I can't handle this.* It would take the real Zorro to tame this tiger.

"You tell Jade Harper that nobody dumps Daisy Donovan. Nobody that doesn't end up regretting it. And it goes double for her. She and Suz and Mackenzie Hawthorne aren't the queen bees of BC, even if they think they are. And for some odd reason, I get distinctly brotherly vibes whenever I'm near you. It's really tragic. All kinds of man, and something about you makes me want to pat your head like a puppy. I just don't get it."

She sauntered off, sexy in a white Cinderella ball gown that bordered on safe-for-kiddies-and-somehow-unsafe-for-bachelors. Ty wiped his brow under the gallant black Zorro hat.

"You're smearing the 'stache," Squint told him, suddenly appearing through the crowd.

"Crap!" Ty quit trying to wipe off Daisy's kiss and the sweat on his brow. "Where the hell have you been? And why haven't you got a hold on the princess of peril?" He stared at his pal. "And what is that you're wearing?"

Squint laughed. "*Where* the hell I've been is helping Justin Morant put up another six tables and accompanying chairs. The Haunted H has a much bigger turnout than expected. They also needed about another six dozen wienies for the wienie roast."

"That's nice. Glad you're making yourself useful," Ty growled.

"Why I'm not holding my hot princess is the simplest part of your question. I believe in keeping the lasso loose, brother. But not too loose. I'll be catching up with the Cinderella in question momentarily. Believe me, I'll teach her all about magic pumpkins and wands that do a different kind of magic."

"That's nice," Ty said, still staring at Squint's outrageous getup. "Anyway, what the hell are you?"

"Can't you tell? I'm you." He pointed to the camo bandanna, boots, camo pants, black Kevlar vest and helmet equipped with night-vision goggles. "I'm you going into BUD/S."

"That's so funny I forgot to laugh," Ty said sourly. "It's all fine for you to mock my efforts, since you and Frog are already SEALs. I sense a little rivalry, or perhaps the essence floating through that you don't think I can make it, so mock away. But you're scaring the kiddies and, I might add, their parents. People are looking at you like sharpshooters, assassins and military-grade security were hired for this shindig," he said, keeping his voice low. "At least take off the goggles and hide the artillery, okay?"

"It's a toy," Squint said, shifting the long gun on his back, letting the strap hang over his shoulder. "It's a water cannon, doofus."

"It doesn't matter. Don't you remember what happened? We don't want anyone recalling that someone died here at the last haunted house."

"He wasn't shot," Squint said.

"We don't want any dangerous vibes. Go put it in your truck! And find Daisy before she starts any more trouble!"

"All right, dude. *Cálmate.* Keep your 'stache on. Damn." Squint went off, obviously a bit insulted.

"Hey, mister," a little boy said. "Are you running the dunking booth?"

"Yes. No." Ty grabbed Sam as he meandered by, and shoved him into his place. "The pirate is tending to the water exhibit. Have fun."

Ty trotted off to locate Raggedy Ann, finding her spinning cotton candy onto paper cones. "Can we talk?"

"Talk away. Want some?"

"Uh, no. Thanks." He handed the fluffy stick of puffed pink sugar she gave him to the first kid in line. "From Zorro to you, kid."

"Thanks, mister!"

The boy hurried off.

"That's not how we make profits here. Weren't you the one who believed that the haunted house and bachelors were all BC needed to get back in the black?" Jade said.

He slapped a hundred dollar bill on the wooden ledge of the ice-cream-and-sweets stand. "Can we talk?"

"We're talking now," Jade said, oozing darling and too-sweet-for-tea.

"I want to talk to you alone."

She gazed at him, her green eyes wide. "Will Daisy allow you to? She just came by here with a—"

"That's it." Ty went into the crowd, grabbed Frog, propelled him to the stand. "Robin Hood's robbing the gremlins and warlocks and giving to the kiddies right here. I mean, the ninjas and pint-size ghosts. Make yourself useful and give these tiny customers a good show," he told Frog, tugging Jade out from the booth. He pulled her into the bunkhouse a little unceremoniously, but he was running out of days to break through the ice with this little gal. "There are way too many urchins around here. It's enough to make a single guy nervous as hell."

He dropped onto a sofa, pulled off the Zorro hat and the mask and the one side of the mustache that wasn't painted on. There was just no help for it; he had to do something before he went mad. So he swept Jade into his lap. "Now you listen to me and you listen good. I want nothing to do with Daisy Donovan, and you know it. You're just having a helluva good time teeing me up about it."

"Yes, I am. You deserve every moment of it."

He stared into Jade's dangerously green eyes, which reminded him of a hidden forest, and wished he knew of a forest somewhere to drag her off to. The closest one was near Bridesmaids Creek's creek, and it was far too cold to drag her there. She didn't fight—or even move— to get out of his lap, so he decided she liked being with him more than she was saying.

"You smell good. Like cotton candy."

"And peach ice cream and sprinkles and hot cocoa and popcorn. Sexy stuff." Jade looked at him. "I wasn't being honest. You're a really hunky Zorro."

He looked at her, suspicious. "Now you tell me."

"Couldn't tell you with Daisy hanging on to your face."

That sounded like an opening he couldn't pass up. "Okay, you hang on to my lips, and I'll probably get the message."

To his astonishment, Jade kissed him, long and slow and sweet, taking a tantalizingly hot tour of his mouth. Ty's brain blew a short circuit that fried The Plan and all his good sense and intentions in one fiery explosion.

"Get the message?" she asked, pulling back to study him.

He certainly had gotten something. "I'm not quite sure. If you do that again, I can probably—"

She put a finger against his lips. "You're leaving in, what, eight days? Nine?"

"Yeah. Wanna give me a private going-away party?" He wrapped his arms around her, mashing her closer to him, sighing against her neck. Wondered if he dared unzip the Raggedy Ann dress. "God, you taste better than cotton candy. Do it again."

"My point was, you're leaving. And according to The Plan I've heard so much about, the last thing you need are entanglements and issues back home when you go. That's straight from the BUD/S training bible, or the code you live by, or something, isn't it?"

The heat she was causing by sitting on him was just about unbearable. Even his eyeballs were heating and his brain was smoking, fogging his heretofore perfect reserve around Jade. "I can handle any issue you throw at me, doll face."

"How punny of you."

"No. You are a doll face, even when you're not Raggedy Ann. I don't care what you're wearing, you make my brain go bye-bye just by looking at you."

She stared at him. "What has gotten into you?"

"You," he said, thick desire terminating his normal inhibition. "You're in my blood, and I don't know why the hell I never realized it before."

Those dark green eyes stayed on him. "You know this is a very bad idea," Jade stated.

"It may be," Ty said, "but that's exactly what makes me so convinced I need to take this walk on the wild side."

"So you want to make love to me?"

He hadn't gotten that far in his thinking, but as soon as she mentioned it, he went straight up like the pirate sword his buddy had been carting around. "The question is, do you want me to make love to you?"

She straddled him, kissing him, and the bits of his poor Jade-addled brain hot-wired right into another dimension. All he could think of was that he better kiss the daylights out of her before she changed her mind, before she convinced herself that this really was the bad idea of all bad ideas.

But she rocked against him instead, and he slipped his hands under the blue dress and white apron, nearly dying at the sweet feel of her butt cheeks in his palms after he'd been surreptitiously lusting after them all this time. Jade moved against his crotch, getting as close as she could, her kisses matching his for urgency and passion. He held her tight, crushing her fanny against him, his tongue sweeping inside her mouth, tasting peppermint and even a little sweet cotton candy. He wanted her more than he wanted his next breath, but no way was he going to do anything to scare her away. Talking about making love and actually doing it—well, a man couldn't take anything for granted, no matter how much he wanted inside the soft, welcoming heaven he knew Jade would be.

"Well?" she asked softly.

"Well what?" He stared, mesmerized and still, into her big eyes, hardly daring to believe that this moment was actually coming true for him. Holding Jade was so much more amazing than his dreams had ever been.

"Are you going to make love to me or not?"

He gulped. "What about all that business about me leaving, and The Plan?"

She began unbuttoning his shirt. "I'm a big girl."

Dear God, she was, a big, beautiful girl. Nothing like the playmate with whom he'd roughhoused. "I don't want to—"

"Leave me holding the bag?" Jade kissed his mouth, tracing his lips with her tongue. "Will you quit being a gentleman and act a little more like your costume?"

He blinked. "Just to clarify—"

She got up, dragged him to his bedroom. Closed and locked the door. "Listen up, cowboy. You brought your buddies here to settle the ladies. You need to do your part."

"That part of The Plan was about bringing eligible, marriage-seeking bachelors to BC." She had his shirt off now and was working on the bottom half of his costume, and Ty wondered if he could survive for the next six months without this woman.

"I'm not looking for marriage. I'm not looking for anything but a little dangerous costume sex and maybe some playacting. Can you handle that?"

"I can sure man up to the occasion." He caught her hands in his. "And then what?"

"And then you go off and do your thing, and I do mine." Jade smiled. "You'll tell your buddies you nailed Raggedy Ann, and they'll be totally impressed. I'm just hoping my Zorro fantasy lives up to the real thing."

Well, there was a challenge a man just had to accept. Ty slowly unzipped the blue dress, pushed it down over her arms, dropped that and the white apron to the floor, nearly asphyxiated from the desire clogging his throat. She was perfect. Long and lean and tall, just like he'd imagined. Peach-sized breasts, freckles in some spectacularly sexy places and a navel he planned to get very familiar with.

After he licked every centimeter of that deliciously heart-shaped ass. "Come here, doll face. Zorro's going to show you exactly why his blade made him a legend."

Chapter Five

Jade was horrified when she awakened in the bunkhouse, realizing that Zorro was gone, and maybe so was her reputation as a Haunted H volunteer. She slipped her costume back on, annoyed that she'd dozed off—but then again, those moments in Ty's arms had been wonderful. She'd finally managed to seduce Ty Spurlock. How long had she waited for the right moment to kiss that footloose cowboy? Forever. When the opportunity had finally presented itself, no way would she have passed it up, even if she felt silly wearing painted-on freckles. A pass by the mirror showed that the freckles were a thing of the past—Ty had kissed her senseless, every centimeter of her body. A few dot-on lip liner freckles were no match for that man's roving, heated kisses.

He was dynamite in bed, and she'd fibbed like mad, telling him he wasn't sexy in his costume. Protecting herself, putting up barriers that, thankfully, she'd let down just in time. Her body sang with delirious joy at the amazing things he'd done to her.

The thought of Ty leaving for BUD/S was terrifying in a way—but she'd sold him the notion that they would go their separate ways, no strings attached.

"And I'm sticking to that story, because it's the only one I've got." Jade slipped out the back so no one would notice where she'd been for the hour she'd been gone. The haunting was still in full swing, though the kiddies were looking a trifle spent. Parents began strolling with their tired children toward the massive parking lot manned by BC volunteers. She returned to the ice-cream stand, picking up her duties smoothly from Frog, who'd been doing a creditable job of twirling cotton candy. "Thanks for working my shift. Head off and have some fun, Frog."

He grinned at her. "I saw Ty go by a while ago, and he's missing half his mustache again. It's about time someone gave that cocky dude something to do with his mouth besides run it."

"I can't imagine what you mean." Jade handed a couple of mugs of hot cocoa to a young couple who looked exhausted by their small fry's evening out. But they smiled at her as they left, mentioning how much fun they'd had at the haunted house, and a funny arrow of longing hit Jade as she watched them walk away, pushing their stroller, enjoying their cocoa and the togetherness with their family.

She was never going to have that. To have a family she would need a man, and the only man she'd ever loved was Zorro, er, Ty Spurlock. All that business about them going their separate ways was just big talk to get him loosened up enough to say yes to her seduction of him.

"Well, I suppose I'll go see if I can hunt up a pair of lips to snack on. All this sweet stuff has made me hungry," Frog said, winking. "Your smile is a little crooked, Raggedy Ann, but I guess that won't come as a surprise, since you disappeared into the bunkhouse with Ty."

"Mind your own business, Frog." She tried to scowl at him, but he was so pleased that he thought he'd guessed her secret. She was too happy to frown, anyway; her heart was singing one minute, diving into uncertainty the next.

Frog ambled off, and her mother leaned over and whispered, "Daisy knows you and Ty disappeared together somewhere. She hung out here for a good half hour to see when you'd return."

"For all she knows, I was on parking-lot duty." Jade didn't care what the woman thought—Ty was never going to be Daisy's. Jade had caught him first, and she was going to keep him for the few days he had left in BC. Daisy could go jump in the creek.

"I tried to tell her you were helping with other stands," Betty said, "but she seems to have radar where Ty is concerned."

"Tough." Smiling, Jade helped her mother close down the stand, packing away the food and the condiments and serving utensils to take back to the ice-cream shop in town.

All was going well until an ostentatiously large Hummer limo pulled into the Haunted H grounds. Robert Donovan got out, and the limo slipped off, leaving him surveying the running tots and happy visitors with a frown. Standing about six-four, Robert was a man who struck fear into the hearts of many. He had black hair threaded with gray, massive shoulders, and boots that seemed too large to be real.

"Don't look now, but the destroyer of light and happiness has arrived," Jade told her mother.

There were still about two hundred guests at the park, lingering because of the romantic stars and pretty strung lights, and probably because they were having a grand time at a fun family event that had been closed for years.

"He's only here to make trouble," Betty said. "You can count on that."

"I suppose I'll take him a cup of hot cocoa, since we haven't emptied the pot out yet. Maybe the sweetness will keep him from his mission of mischief." It was the only possibly reason he could be here. The man had done everything he could to block the Haunted H from reopening, and so had his daughter. Which was kind of strange, since Daisy had been working the carnival to-night. Jade frowned as she walked toward Robert with the cocoa.

She was beaten to him by Suz Hawthorne. "Come to spoil our success, Robert?" Suz demanded. Her pe-tite frame was a good foot and some shorter than the man she'd accosted. But Suz was fearless. Jade hurried to her friend's side.

"What success?" Robert looked at both women, his eyes eagle-stern, his hawklike nose somehow express-ing his disdain. "This isn't a success. There are so many code violations here the Haunted Heap won't be open long." He smirked. "Be a good girl and go get your big sister. I have something I want to tell Mackenzie."

Suz drew herself up. "My sister and I are partners and co-owners. You can say whatever needs to be said to me, or not say it at all."

"My words can come just as easily in the form of a legal complaint."

Suz shrugged. "It's your money. I'm not interrupt-ing Mackenzie's big night just so you can spout off. You can see we're a huge success and you're just ticked as ticked can be."

Ty's hand suddenly braced Jade at her back, his other hand supporting Suz at her shoulders. "You bugging my best girls, Donovan?"

Robert frowned. "What the hell business is it of yours?"

"Just as much as it is yours. As far as I can see, unless you've bought a ticket, you're trespassing." Ty jerked his head toward the Hummer limo idling a discreet distance away in the outbound lane. "Overcompensate much?"

Robert's eyes flamed. A slight gasp escaped Jade, and Ty's hand moved from her back to her shoulder, supporting her as he was Suz.

"You tell your sister," Robert said to Suz, "that this dump is closed. There'll be no more of this once I file a cease-and-desist motion. According to the petition drive, a great many BC residents don't want this grubby little flea market bringing crime and vagrants to our quiet town, and I believe the law will be on my side." He looked triumphant.

"The only people who signed that petition against us were people you threatened with some kind of financial wipeout. Like Mssr. Unmatchmaker," Jade said. "Anyway, most all of BC is here. Including your daughter."

Robert frowned, his massive forehead looking as if divots had suddenly been furrowed in the granite. He opened his mouth to speak, but a sudden scream from someone in the crowd cut him off.

"Call an ambulance!" a voice cried.

"Is there a doctor here?" someone else yelled.

Suz, Jade and Ty ran toward the people surrounding Betty's ice-cream stand. The older woman looked terrified.

"He was fine a minute ago!" Betty exclaimed, pointing to a man lying on the ground. "He bought cocoa!"

Jade looked at the cocoa in her hands, which she'd never given Robert, and glanced down at the prone figure. People were bent over him, trying to give him assistance and checking his pulse.

"He's dead," Sheriff Dennis said, kneeling at the man's side.

"It was the cocoa!" someone in the crowd whispered.

They all gazed at the ice-cream-and-sweets stand, and at Betty, who appeared confused and frightened.

"It was *not* the cocoa," Jade called loudly, raising the cup. "This is cocoa I poured myself from right here, at our family's stand. Our own home recipe, I might add. I was taking Mr. Donovan a cup," she said, glancing at Robert. "There's nothing wrong with the cocoa."

People gazed at her, suspicious and nervous that they might have consumed something poisonous from the little stand. Jade raised the cup again, and with about a hundred pairs of eyes on her, drank every bit of it.

Silence fell, eerie compared to the laughter and joy that had marked the evening all night long. Even the children were still and silent, confused by what was happening.

"It's clear to see," Robert Donovan began, "that this repeat performance, just like so many years ago—"

"Oh, for crying out loud, Donovan." Sheriff Dennis rose from his abandoned attempts at CPR. He placed his jacket over the victim's face out of respect. "Don't start that crap, with this poor soul not gone from this life a full five minutes." He barked at his deputy to get the coroner on the double.

People still eyed Jade, convinced that any second she'd fall to the ground dead.

Then, to her everlasting thankfulness, Ty's voice split the tension. "Betty, pour me a big-ass mug of that cocoa, would you?"

Gratitude hit Jade square in her heart. She watched her mother's hands shake as she poured and handed a cup to Ty. He raised it to Robert. "Bottoms up," he said, and finished it off, smacking his lips. "Best cocoa I ever had, just the way it's always been, Mrs. Harper. Ever since I was a boy, I looked forward to coming home on cold days to your house. I always knew there'd be a pot of hot cocoa and chocolate-chip cookies waiting in your kitchen. Did I ever thank you for that?"

Betty finally smiled, timidly but thankfully. Jade felt something bloom inside her, something that had been there a long time as just a tiny seed, but now blossomed into feelings much more deep. She smiled at Ty, who winked at her.

He turned to the sheriff. "Why don't you get Donovan to donate his vehicle for a couple of hours to haul this unfortunate soul over to the medical examiner's place?"

"I'll do no such thing!" Robert looked as if he might strip a gear, relaxing only a little when he saw his daughter, Daisy, standing at the edge of the crowd. "Honey, you need to come away from this place. It's dangerous."

"Nobody's going anywhere," Sheriff Dennis said. "My deputies will see to that. Until the M.E. arrives and gives us a preliminary guess as to how this individual died, everybody's staying right here. My deputies will see that you're comfortable as can be. Bridesmaids Creek is known for its hospitality. I'd say the appropriate medical personnel will be here any second, so relax, folks."

Betty began unpacking her stand, setting everything back up so that people could have something to eat and to feed their kids.

"I'd better help Mom." Jade looked up at Ty. "Thanks for everything."

He smiled at her. "I wouldn't miss tweaking Robert Donovan for the world. You know that."

"I heard that." Daisy frowned, suddenly appearing at his side. "You're just under Jade's spell, Ty Spurlock. My dad's trying to help BC, while the Harpers and the Hawthornes are trying to destroy it."

"You didn't look like anybody was hurting you tonight, Daisy," Jade said. "Who gave you the assignment of painting faces, anyway?"

"No one." Daisy sniffed. "I just wanted to participate."

"Why? You're too much like your father to want us to succeed. Was the goal to frighten off our customers?" Jade was too mad to be polite.

"We don't have to frighten off your customers. You do such a good job of *killing* them off." Daisy huffed, then went to stand beside her father.

"Pay no attention to her." Ty put his arm around Jade. "Let's figure out a way to keep these folks occupied with happy thoughts."

Jade went with Ty as he rounded up the guys, determined to put the best face possible on the Haunted H. But even she knew that after what had just happened, it would be almost impossible to dispel the rumor that something was very, very wrong in Bridesmaids Creek.

Chapter Six

Ty walked across to the bunkhouse, dead tired and ready to tuck in for the night. After the events of the evening, he couldn't help worrying that he was leaving his little town when it needed him most. The Donovans were definitely up to no good, and they had a pretty firm grip on BC. Jade and Suz and Mackenzie were tough, ready to face up to the Donovans, and they had a lot of community support. But there were still people who would fall in with the Donovans simply because money bought power—and silence.

Jade walked inside the bunkhouse behind him, following him to his room. "Thanks for sticking up for Mom. And our business."

He hadn't done much. Ty looked at Jade, tossed his hat on the dresser, tugged off his belt. "I didn't do anything anybody else wouldn't have done."

"You kept the Donovans from completely decimating our business."

"Maybe. For tonight." He shook his head. "I've got a bad feeling the haunted house may be damaged for good. All that hard work the Hawthornes, you and your family, the town and my guys put in trying to build BC into something better." Fury boiled inside him. "The Donovans just don't give up."

She walked over to him, caressed his cheek. "Ty, there's only so much you can do. We'll be fine here in BC."

He wished he knew that was true. Jade stood too close, clouding his senses. Ty relaxed into her palm, allowing himself to take the comfort she offered. He was angry for her sake, too. He'd seen the distress on Betty's face—and there was Jade, immediately stepping up to defend her mother. These two women gave constantly of themselves to BC—but they were like tiny acorns standing up to a giant, mighty oak for space. Robert Donovan was too ruthless, and the Harpers very fragile and defenseless.

Ty stepped away from Jade. "The sheriff said it appears the visitor died of a plain old garden-variety heart attack. So this time we have a conclusive cause of death, unlike the first time." The first death would never be solved, and people had long memories. He supposed that was why he felt so strongly about doing what he could to raise BC from the ground, because he knew what Donovan had done to his adopted father with rumors and scandalmongering.

And now it might be happening again. "I'm running out of ideas to stop Donovan."

Jade plopped down on his bed. "Look. You've got to think about packing that locker over there," she said, pointing to where he'd been gathering up everything he needed for training. "You need to think only of your future, and getting into the SEALs. We're going to be fine here, Ty. I promise. We're a pretty resilient group. You know that."

"Yeah." He took a long look at Jade, tried not stare at her face, drink her in. She was so optimistic, so spunky. He'd hate to see all that ironed out of her by Donovan. It had happened to his father. Gradually, even resilience could be worn down by continued pounding, like rock worn away by the relentless sea.

Then again, Ty had his own team in place. The thought wasn't exactly heartening, but it was something. "Where are the three musketeers?"

Jade smiled at him, melting his heart. "They're about to rumble with Daisy's gang. I think Frog said they were going to duel—"

"What?" Ty stared at Jade. "Why didn't you tell me sooner?" He crammed his hat back on, grabbed his belt, thrusting it though his belt loops as he hurried to the front door.

She followed him. "I didn't tell you because I knew you'd do this."

"Do what?" He peered out the window, seeing that the last people had packed up their stands and deserted the Haunted H for the night. Hardly anybody was left on the ranch, and a full moon shone overhead—a perfect night for a full-on squabble between rival factions. "What am I doing?"

"Rushing off to play peacemaker." Jade dragged him from the window. "They're big boys. They can handle themselves. That's why you brought them here, right? To handle things?"

"I'm not sure why I brought them here anymore." Ty realized Jade was bent on keeping him away from the fight. "What's really going on?"

"What do you mean?"

She gave him such an innocent look that Ty belatedly

realized she'd been sent to waylay him with a little faux seduction. He grinned. She was so charming and darling, thinking she had him right where she wanted him.

Well, if she was going to go to the trouble to seduce him, he might as well show up for her efforts. He pulled her into his arms. "It doesn't matter what the *tres* knuckleheads are up to. I'd rather find out what you're up to." He kissed her, taking his time with her mouth, enjoying sinking into her soft lips over and over.

The best part was how hungrily Jade kissed him back. Ty's head swam, and momentarily he lost his place in his own plan. "Hey," he said, pulling back to gaze into her eyes.

"Yes?" Those eyes had nothing but sweet shyness in them, and Ty wanted to surrender completely to her.

"You're supposed to be keeping me busy."

"I'm doing my best, cowboy."

That she was. All kinds of attraction was steamrolling him. It was killing him not to let his desire for Jade completely entice him into her scheme.

Her hands roamed across his back, and Ty's heart rate kicked into high gear. Whatever she was hiding, it was something she wanted to keep hidden for sure. She kissed along his jaw, made her way back to his mouth. Ty closed his eyes, hoped he wouldn't black out from denying himself the pleasure of Jade's temptress act.

"Okay, little lady." He set her away from him. "I'm giving you an A for effort. I'm not the kind of schmo who falls for a few kisses." He pushed his shirt back into his jeans, since it had worked loose thanks to Jade's clever little hands.

"Yes, you are. You're exactly the kind who falls for a few kisses."

This was dangerous ground. "Yeah, well, not anymore. Take me to this rumble you're trying to keep me from."

"No."

"I'll find it myself."

She blocked the door with her curvaceous body, flattened like a protective shield to keep him from leaving. "You won't."

Ty wanted to press Jade up against that door and kiss the daylights out of her, but she was trying so hard to waylay him that he had to see how far she'd take this newfound protectiveness. "I'll want more than a kiss or two if I'm not going to join the fun, cupcake."

She wrinkled her nose. "Thickheaded, much?"

Ty grinned. "If you can't stand the heat, don't wander into the kitchen. Now lead me to trouble."

"You're leaving for BUD/S soon. You need to be in good shape, not all busted up from a fight."

Ty stared at the most kissable mouth in town. "I've played this totally wrong."

"What do you mean?"

"I brought the three doorknobs here to settle the ladies. What I didn't realize was that it was the men in this town who needed settling." He couldn't get over how sweet she'd felt in his arms. Every man needed that kind of sweetness in his life—then there'd be no rumbling. "Daisy's gang of five creepos. They need women. Then there'll be no fighting, just five happy family men tied down by diapers and wedding rings."

Jade locked the door, turned the bolt. Stayed right on her marker, not moving an inch.

"You can't stay there forever, sweetheart," Ty said. "This standoff between you and me is going to end one way or the other. Either I go join the fun, or I pick you up in my big, strong arms and lock you in my room so no one can interrupt what I'm going to do to you." He couldn't imagine what the ruckus was about, but he could hear shouts and smack talking. Jade looked more worried by the moment, glancing behind her at one particularly loud yell.

For a moment he thought she might relent and allow him to leave. She settled a meaningful gaze on him instead.

"I want a baby."

Ty stepped back a pace, stunned. "What does that have to do with me?"

"I want you to give me a child."

He blinked, took in her very serious expression. "That's a pretty good tactic, beautiful. You nearly gave me heart failure. But I'm not falling for it, so move your sweet little buns away from that door. My brothers need me."

She shook her head. "I want a baby, and you're the man who can help me."

He smiled, staggered by her charming ploy to keep him in the bunkhouse. "Well, of course I can help you. But as we both know, I'm leaving. I don't have time for romance and nonsense, and I'm not getting married, so—"

"I didn't say I wanted to marry you," Jade said, annoyed. "You're never coming back to BC, so you're the perfect man for what I need."

He went to the playbook to save himself. "SEALs are advised to get all their affairs wrapped up and put their private lives at rest—"

"That's fine. You go be a SEAL, and I'll be a mother."

Jade's eyes softened. "Ty, you weren't here for years. You only came home to save BC. You were going to ride in, disperse some Prince Charmings, leave behind some happy newlyweds to blossom into families, thus seeding the town with more BC-friendly citizens, then ride off into the Technicolor sunset."

He could hear a full-blown rumble erupting around the bunkhouse. "I wish I could help you, but I can't."

"You can't get me pregnant?"

"Well, sure I could." Ty was pretty confident he had the right stuff for that, if she was inclined to give him a shot. "I could probably do it in one try," he boasted.

Jade shook her head. "Please wait a moment while I remind myself that your cockiness is one of the reasons I chose you to be the father of my child."

He cupped her face with his palm. "You chose me because your ovaries clearly recognize good genes." He stroked her soft skin, thinking there was nothing he'd rather do than toss her into his bed and make long, slow love to her again. "However, what would Betty think if I knocked up her only daughter and left town?"

"My mother will be delighted to finally have a grand-child." Jade moved his hand away. "And it's ovary."

A siren shrieked outside and Ty gazed into Jade's eyes, wondering what was going on that she was so willing to keep him out of it with the intriguing notion of sex and fatherhood. He studied her. "Ovary?"

"That's right. I only have one."

He pondered this. "So you're looking for a mighty big gun to hit the target."

She laughed out loud. "To go with your big mouth. Really? You're that cocky?"

He shrugged. "One man's cocky is another man's confidence. Move away from the door, angel face."

"You're turning me down?"

He scoffed. "Of course I'm turning you down. You're just trying to keep me away from a good old-fashioned brawl. The whole premise of you getting knocked up and me leaving my child here with no father is absurd. Which I think you know." He leaned in for a kiss, then scooted her away from the door after he'd lingered over her lips. "Nice try, though."

Jade moved. "You brought your friends here to populate the town. I'll pitch my plan to Sam."

Ty stopped cold, his hand on the knob, at the word *plan*. Even Jade had a plan—everybody in BC did—and he should have factored that in. Instead, he'd seen her as a sweet, sexy woman he was leaving behind because he had no other choice—nothing could interfere with *his* Plan. "Sam?"

Jade nodded. "He's a wonderful man. You wouldn't have brought him to BC if you didn't know that beyond a shadow of a doubt."

Ty couldn't deny it, so he didn't bother.

"Besides which, he's not a bad kisser," Jade teased. "Or so I hear."

Something hard hit Ty in the gut, the same punch that had hit him the day he'd seen her walking into The Wedding Diner on Sam's arm. "Sam is a great guy."

"Obviously."

Ty didn't consider himself a jealous man—he just wasn't. And he wasn't going to be today. "Well, whatever you have to do, sugar," he said, and headed out the door to find his friends and the trouble they'd cooked up.

He was certain he'd left bigger trouble behind, redheaded trouble looking to give him a surefire coronary. Yet despite Jade's plan, and her sassy little mouth and hot body, there definitely wasn't going to be a baby, at least not from his gene pool.

The little lady was going to have go swimming elsewhere.

Chapter Seven

Jade followed Ty, having stalled him as long as she could. She didn't want him joining the fight, or getting involved with the ongoing trouble brewing in BC. The conflict could go on forever, thanks to the Donovans and their wealth.

Ty needed to leave town. His desire to get into the SEALs was part of who he was; he'd talked about it, prepared his body and spirit for it for years. Part of the reason he'd brought Frog, Sam and Squint here was because he'd gotten to know them on the rodeo circuit, where they'd drifted after their time in the SEALs, still wanting action and to be part of a community, a brotherhood. To be fair, Ty had never wanted to settle in Bridesmaids Creek. Life could be slow here, not the adventure he longed for. Jade understood that—everybody in BC did. They were all rooting for him to go off and achieve his dreams.

In Bridesmaids Creek, achieving your dreams made you a hero, a legend. It wasn't just the men, either—women dreamed as big as the sky, too. Even Daisy had dreams—although they were counterpoint to what was best for BC, at least in Jade's opinion.

Maybe the scuffle was over. Daisy and her gang of

five hangers-on faced off against Squint, Frog and Sam just as Justin Morant came over, holding one of his four babies. Mackenzie Hawthorne Morant stood by her husband, pushing a stroller with the other three tucked inside under soft, warm blankets. Jade's mother hovered protectively nearby, doing her best grandmother-in-training routine.

Sheriff Dennis looked crossly at the men eyeing each other, facing off in the light from the barn's kid-friendly haunted-house decorations, pumpkin-shaped globes and a few strings of smiling ghosts mixed among the white, twinkling lights.

"What's going on?" Ty demanded, and Jade hurried up behind him, fully intending to drag him away if any punches were thrown. Under no circumstances was he going to SEAL training messed up from fighting.

"Your band of merry men," Daisy said, "jumped my guys."

"We didn't jump them," Frog said. "We just played a friendly prank."

"Friendly? How friendly?" Ty demanded.

Daisy's friends glowered at Ty's buddies. Jade could feel hostility oozing from every pore of all the men. *Testosterone,* she thought, disgusted. *There's far too much of it in BC.* And the smell of horse manure was really strong, so strong Jade raised a hand over her nose for a moment.

"Nothing to cause a ruckus over," Sam said. "Donovan's doing his best to ruin a good thing here. We just want these fellows to know we're keeping an eye on them."

"How much of an eye?" Ty asked. "What did you do?"

His friends smiled, pleased with themselves.

"We just gave them a small roll in the dirt," Squint said.

Jade's eyes widened as she realized the smell of manure was coming from Daisy's gang. "Oh, no. You didn't!"

Frog laughed. "We did. And it was awesome!"

That was too much for Daisy's friends. The five men leaped onto Frog, Squint and Sam. Justin handed the baby to Betty and jumped into the fray, and before Jade could get a hand on Ty, he'd thrown himself into the fight. Fists and curses flew.

"Aren't you going to do something?" Jade asked Sheriff Dennis.

"Nope. In fact, I'm heading into the kitchen. Betty had a couple of cinnamon cakes put by for the workers, and that means me." He went off, whistling.

Jade looked at Mackenzie and Betty. "We have to stop them."

"They brought it on themselves," Betty said.

"Mom!" Jade stared at her mother. "You don't condone fighting!"

Betty sighed. "Let's let the fellows sort it out. I'm taking the babies inside before they get cold."

Jade's mouth fell open. "Mackenzie, Ty's supposed to leave in a few days to try to make it into the SEALs. He came home to save your Hanging H ranch, and your Haunted H business. Tell them to stop fighting!"

Mackenzie, her dearest and best friend going back years and years, shook her head. "Ty isn't going to thank you if you go rushing in there all mother hen."

That was true. Jade scoffed in resignation. "Why are men so stupid? What is this solving?" It looked as if the men were having the time of their lives, acting like children. "Women should rule the world," she muttered.

"We do. Quietly." Betty made sure all the babies were comfortable, and pushed the pram toward the big, lovely old Hawthorne house. "These men have brought BC back from the dead. We're just getting life breathed back into them. If they want to fight, I say let's go warm up some cocoa and cider. And find bandages."

Jade glanced at Ty, worried. No one seemed to understand the importance of him not getting his clock cleaned right before he left town. What if he broke something, was seriously injured?

This was too stupid—and she hadn't exactly succeeded in her mission of keeping Ty out of this fight once she knew it was going down. He hadn't bought the let's-get-pregnant bombshell she'd tried to waylay him with. She couldn't take the testosterone overload a second longer.

"That's enough!" Jade strode over to Daisy, who was watching and encouraging her guys, clapping when one of them landed a good blow. Jade grabbed her by that fabulous chocolate hair, dragged her to the ground and sat on her. "Make them stop, Daisy. Call them off."

"No way!"

"Now. Or I cut off your hair. I mean it."

"You wouldn't!"

"I *would*." Jade looked up as she realized Mackenzie stood next to her. "Got any scissors?"

"Sure." Her friend handed her a large pair of shears.

"Why do you have these?" Jade asked, ignoring Daisy as she suddenly squalled something that wasn't very ladylike.

"It wasn't hard to tell where this was going." Mackenzie laughed. "You had blood in your eye for Daisy. I figured it was either douse her in the creek, dunk her in a horse trough or take scissors to that pretty hair. I came prepared. Besides which, I was working the balloons at one point tonight and I needed scissors to cut the ribbons."

"Excellent. Call them off, Daisy." Jade bounced on her to emphasize the words.

"No. The Hawthornes are not the princesses of Bridesmaids Creek. Suz and Mackenzie aren't royalty around here! We're going to buy this dump, and —"

"You never learn." Jade picked up a good-size handful of chocolate locks and snipped them right next to Daisy's scalp.

The scream her victim let out was bloodcurdling— and so were some of the words she leveled at Jade.

"Call them off!" Jade commanded.

Daisy tried to buck her off, but Jade was too strong, and Mackenzie helped hold her still. "I shouldn't get involved in this. I have four daughters to set an example for," Mackenzie said. "Cut fast."

Jade picked up an indiscriminate handful from the back and clipped it off. Daisy was going to look like she'd fallen under a lawn mower.

The scream Daisy unleashed this time was probably heard in the next county. Jade winced, but the men quit fighting, turning to stare at the three women.

"What are you doing, Jade?" Ty demanded.

"Just playing a friendly prank," she said sweetly. "Nothing to cause a ruckus over."

"Help me!" Daisy yelled at her friends.

"No," Jade said, brandishing the pointy scissors. "Not

unless you want me to take another, oh, six inches out of Daisy's pride and joy."

When she was satisfied that no one was going to try to save Daisy, she nodded. "No more fighting tonight. You look ridiculous, every one of you." She glared at Ty, so he'd know she was including him, even though he looked hot as the dickens all roughed up and tough from battle. But it was the wrong battle. "And you stink to high heaven."

All the men seemed to finally realize that manure and testosterone was a bad combination. Not women-friendly in the least.

"This isn't going to be settled tonight, but Daisy, you and your father are on the wrong side. One of these days you're going to figure that out." Jade flexed the scissors in the air with a snicking sound to keep Daisy quiet, and it worked like a charm. "I want you and your gang off this property right now, or I won't be responsible for the buzz cut I'm going to give you. All of you." She snicked the scissors in the air again. "Got it?"

"Fine," Daisy said, "but just know I live to fight another day. Probably tomorrow."

"Fine. Tomorrow I'll have had some sleep, and I'll be ready with something better than scissors. Maybe green hair dye. You'd look good as a lettuce-head, matching that money you're always bragging about. Or maybe a bleached blonde."

"Witch," Daisy spit, leaping to her feet when Jade let her up. "You won't win. You're the one on the wrong side. You have no man, Jade Harper, and no hope of one. You'll live and die in this town a spinster, or marry nothing more than a farmer."

Jade smiled. "Frankly, I'd be proud to marry a farmer.

That might not be big enough for you, but the farming, small-town life suits me fine, Daisy. It's the reason you've never really fitted in here after all these years—you and your father are trying to change us into something we're not. The grand Donovan vision."

She handed the scissors back to Mackenzie. Satisfied that the brawl was over and no one was going to be seriously injured for the night—and annoyed as heck with Ty for getting involved when he knew very well he shouldn't—she walked toward her truck. She'd seen blood on his face and his lip was split open—that mouth that had kissed her not too long ago, kissed her senseless—and her temper simmered at the stupidity of it all.

It was time to go home—before she let fly all over that rugged cowboy.

"Hang on," Ty said, looking as if he was about to hop into the passenger side before she could even turn the key in the ignition. "I want to talk to you about this having-a-baby and marrying-a-farmer business."

Jade shook her head. "I'm done talking. Don't you even dream of getting into my truck after you've been rolling in horse crap. I tried to save you, but no. You had to go all Rambo."

"Oh, no, little lady. You're going to patch me up."

She was too steamed to pay attention to his plea for attention. "You're fine, barely scratched. Go home."

He grinned. "You tried to save me from myself, and I'm ready to express my gratitude."

TY WASN'T LETTING Jade leave without him. He wasn't about to let his fiery little friend get away, so he talked her into hanging around while he took first a hose-off in the barn, then a shower in the bunkhouse, and finally hauled ass into her truck before she could change her mind. When he'd seen her straddling Daisy like a too-tight saddle, snipping off chunks of her hair, he'd nearly had heart failure. No man ever envisioned a full-on catfight without getting a little chuckle out of it, but Jade hadn't been messing around and he hadn't laughed.

No—he'd realized he was totally, irretrievably falling for her. She'd been trying to defend him, and Bridesmaids Creek, and why he'd never realized she was such a devoted heroine, he didn't know. What he did know was that everything had changed tonight. Just sitting in the truck with her as she drove toward her house had his heart hammering and his jeans way too tight in a certain area.

Jade Harper was the woman of his heart.

"So I've been considering your offer—" he began.

"Rescinded," she interrupted.

"Not so fast," he said, his tone soothing. "We need to get back to the single-ovary issue. I believe I'm your man."

She shook her head, visibly aggravated with him. "You are not my man."

"Well, you certainly don't want a farmer."

"I would want a farmer, if he understood hearth and home, and that fighting never solves anything."

"Says the woman who just gave Daisy Donovan the haircut from hell."

"She needed that," Jade said. "She's had that coming for years."

He wanted to laugh, but held back to keep himself out of trouble. "Let's talk about that baby you want. Or was that just a ploy to keep me from the fight?"

She turned into the drive of the small farmhouse

where she and Betty lived. "It was a ploy, and I do want a baby."

"So the offer's still open."

"No. It's not." She got out of the truck. "You know what? This is so not a good idea. You can walk back, since I didn't invite you into my truck in the first place."

He swooped her up, deposited her in the porch swing and sat down beside her. "Not until we finish the discussion you started earlier."

"It's late." Jade scowled at him, her expression clearly visible in the soft lights that decorated the wraparound porch.

"There's an important rule about never going to bed mad," Ty said, reaching out to twine a strand of her hair around his finger. It was so soft, and she was so soft. He was dying to hold her again.

"I'm fine with going to bed mad. I just want to go to bed." Jade removed his hand from her hair. "Go away."

"I'll be completely out of your hair in just a few days," Ty said. "Let's stay friends."

"Ty, you don't understand. We're sort of friends, the way we always were because we're both from here. But you need to go, and I need to stay." She looked sad. "Wherever you go, you'll find trouble, I have no doubt of that."

She went inside, abandoning him. Ty thought he'd utterly struck out until the door opened again and she came out with a damp cloth.

"Wipe your mouth," she said, "I don't want you bleeding all over the porch. It's been freshly painted."

It had been; he could smell the paint, and the whiteness gleamed in the moonlight and lamplight. Garlands of pine twined around every banister, decorated with red ribbons. A big wreath hung on the door, very festive in the chilly weather. He dabbed at his mouth where it felt as if he'd split it again from grinning at Jade, and she sighed, reaching out to take the cloth from him, pressing it against the spot where he'd taken a slight punch earlier. Strangely, it didn't seem to hurt as much now that Jade was ministering to him.

"You scared me tonight," she said. "I didn't want you fighting, and getting yourself all busted up before you go to training. What would you have done if you've broken a hand or some fingers?"

"It would've sucked," he admitted. "But I had to back up my brothers."

"Those aren't your brothers. Those are your bachelors." Jade shook her head. "The problem with you is that you're always working your plan."

He brightened, caught her hand in his, tossed aside the damp rag she'd been soothing him with and pulled her into his lap. "I'm trying to add you to my plan. Let's get back to your problem. It's more interesting."

"No." She snuggled into him. "Go home, Ty."

"This is my home," he said, looking around the small farmhouse. "I practically grew up here. Betty is like my mother."

"That would make us some kind of siblings, and that would be so weird."

He laughed. "Just because I love your mom doesn't mean I feel brotherly toward you. Let me romance you, Jade. I'll put such a glow on that ovary of yours it'll be spitting out little Tys in no time."

She wrinkled her nose. "Nothing about that convinces me to let you anywhere near my ovary. And can we please stop talking about it?"

"I don't see how you expect me to stop talking about the most interesting proposition I've had in years. Make a baby with a sexy redhead? Hell, yeah!"

She got out of his lap. "Begone."

"I know you want me, Jade Harper. You shouldn't deny yourself the pleasure just because I had to defend the Hanging H from some hardheaded rascals. And may I just remind you one more time that you're the one who did the most damage tonight? Daisy's going to have it in for you like she's never had it in for anyone before. You cut off the thing she loves the most." He laughed, still amused by the spectacle of Jade at work on Daisy's tresses. "You're quite a fighter."

"Men are always so amused by women fighting." Jade shook her head. "I wasn't about to let Daisy get away with hurting Mackenzie and Suz. They're my best friends."

"Besides me."

She looked at him. "Not even close, cowboy."

"So no goodbye party of the sexual variety?"

"As I said, I changed my mind the minute I saw you throw the first punch. What were you thinking?" She put her hands on her hips, and Ty could tell she really was angry with him. "Don't you realize how important your dream is to Bridesmaids Creek? You don't have the right to throw it away on a stupid brawl."

"My dream?"

"We've heard about your SEAL dream for years. We've watched you swim laps in Bridesmaids Creek for hours, watched you run for miles, half the time dragging a tire or something on your back for conditioning. When you came back to BC, we all thought you'd come just to say goodbye. None of us suspected you'd bring eligible bachelors to populate the town, and somehow, that made us think all the more of you." Jade's eyes softened. "You love Bridesmaids Creek almost more than anyone, and the last thing we want is to weigh you down."

He leaned back in the porch swing, astonished. "Weigh me down? This place is my touchstone. It's not a weight."

"Then go achieve your dream. Most of us here will never leave, so we're looking for a hero to live vicariously through."

"You could leave," Ty said.

"I don't want to. I want—" Jade pulled him up from the swing and guided him off the porch "—you to go become a kick-ass SEAL. It's going to be hard, and you need to be in the best shape possible, not all busted up from fighting. Trust me, if you come back in ten years, we'll still be fighting here. It'll be like you're Rip van Winkle and just woke up and nothing changed."

"Jade—"

"And you need to be in great emotional shape, not dragged down by our silly problems. We lived without your guiding hand while you were on the circuit, and we'll be fine without you now. We're tough here, Ty. We don't need you to solve anything for us. So just go."

He stared at her, knowing beyond a shadow of a doubt that the last thing he wanted was to leave this woman behind forever. "Were you serious about having a child?"

"Yes. Absolutely. Betty needs to be a grandmother, and I want to be a mother." For the first time tonight, Jade smiled. "I want exactly what Mackenzie has. And I'll get it, too. Don't worry."

"I'm not exactly worried." He was practically staggered by the thought that she might find a farmer—or

Sam—as soon as he was gone to training, and Ty would come home one day to find a mini-Jade following her mother around. "Damn, Jade, I'm pretty sure you need to let me tickle that ovary of yours."

She pointed to the road. "Go. Be the SEAL this town has always known you could be. We live to brag on our own."

She went inside, closed the door. Ty looked around in the darkness, his heart feeling as if it was bleeding. For a guy who considered himself smooth when it came to the ladies, he hadn't put a dent in Jade's armor against him. Sudden armor, he reminded himself. She sure had seemed eager back at the bunkhouse.

A woman didn't turn off her feelings just because a man got involved in a tiny scuffle, did she? He sank into the porch swing, pondering what the hell had just happened to him. "First she says she wants to have a baby, and I'm the father she's chosen. Then she cuts off Daisy's hair." A moment that had strangely afflicted him with a mixture of horniness, pride and admiration. He went back to his dilemma. "So the hair went poof, and so did Jade's desire to give me a chance to rock that ovary she was so worried about not thirty minutes before." He was so perplexed he felt as if the secure ground he'd been standing on had crumbled.

She *had* tried to keep him from the fight, and she had used sex as a lure. And yet he'd sensed she was very serious underneath the obvious wish to keep him from fighting. Jade wasn't being honest when she blamed her lack of desire to be alone with him on the fact that he'd jumped into the fight; he was going to be a SEAL, and anybody knew SEALs weren't opposed to a little action.

It didn't make sense. But the redhead that gave his

heart severe palpitations of the good kind had definitely closed up on him tighter than a clam, both emotionally and physically.

If he hadn't gone to help his brothers, would Jade really have made love with him? Did she really want his child?

There was only one way to find out.

He got up, banged on her front door.

Chapter Eight

Jade opened the door, which sort of surprised Ty because he wasn't sure that she would.

"Go away," she said.

See, that was exactly why she needed him—she didn't know how sexy she was, and how much she fired him up, sassing him like that. Ty grinned. "Can Jade come out to play?"

"Very funny. That worked when we were kids, but those days are long over."

"And to think I never even tried to play doctor with you, or Spin the Bottle, or any of the other kid games."

"I would have slapped you into next year."

He smiled bigger, couldn't help it. That spunk had his name written all over it. "I need a shotgun rider. Drive out to the old place with me."

Jade's eyes widened. "You're really going to your family home?"

He shrugged. "I'm leaving for a long time, won't be back. I need to rattle the ghosts before I go."

"And you want a fellow rattler."

Ty smiled again. "If anybody is up to the job, beautiful, it's you. Those ghosts don't stand a chance against you."

"So you want me for protection."

He laughed. "Sure. Come on, cowgirl."

She came out onto the porch, closed the door. "You're sure you want to do this?"

"I don't want to at all," he admitted. He hated going out there. It wasn't just the ghosts that got stirred up; it was the memories and the painful knowledge that he hadn't been here for his father when he'd wasted away from grief. "It's best if we face our ghosts. It's the only way to kill them."

"I don't know," Jade said, but she went with him. "There's something wrong with the idea of killing a ghost. I don't think they ever die. Hence, ghost."

These ghosts could die, if time would let them. At least he hoped so. The freight train of sexual attraction he felt for Jade should send them scattering—and he could leave BC with a clear conscience.

At least for a while.

"When's the last time you were there?"

He shrugged as he started the truck. "Whenever I was in town last."

He felt Jade's eyes on him. "You're never curious?"

"Nope. I know it's in good shape because Madame Matchmaker goes out there with a cleaning crew a couple times a month. I get a list as long as your arm whenever there's anything she deems needs to be fixed up." He glanced across at the gorgeous woman in his passenger seat. "Cosette says the place is in museum-quality shape."

A testament to his father's memory. Ty didn't want a single possession of his dad's moved or given away. He wanted to know, every time he returned home, that it was as if he was just coming home again, the way he had when he was a boy, to a father who'd loved him enough to adopt him. Honestly Ty didn't want the ghosts disturbed; he wanted them staying just where they were. The good ghosts, at least.

"You were a good son, Ty," Jade said. "Mom says she felt like you were even a good son to her."

"I tried." He really had tried to be helpful. When his dad had been at work, Betty's house, close to the Hanging H, had been a welcoming place. He'd had the run of it, too. For a kid who might have ended up in an orphanage, he'd been aware of the need to stay in everyone's good graces. He'd wanted so badly to belong.

Then he'd found rodeo, and that family had welcomed him, as well. Suddenly, he didn't have to be the extra addition in everyone's homes; he had a home of his own— the road. His duffel was his portable chest of drawers, his truck his way to a livelihood.

And always, his father told him he was proud of him.

Ty shuddered past the guilt that his father had needed him, and that he'd let him down. "Hey, so about this baby thing. Were you trying to have sex with me because you want a baby, or because you were trying to keep me out of the fight? Tell me the truth and you win the prize."

He stopped the truck in front of his house, gazing at the porch lights, which were on though no one had lived there in years.

"No one just wants a baby," Jade said. "And it was both."

"It's a lot to hang on a guy who's leaving."

"Don't be a wienie." She jumped out of the truck.

"A wienie?" he grumbled to himself. He got out and waited for her to get to his side of the truck.

"I want a baby," Jade said when she got close enough that he could smell her perfume and the scent of sweet cotton candy clinging to her. "But it doesn't have to be you, so don't get yourself in a twist."

He caught her to him. "I am in a twist, and if you say one more word about Sam and your ovary, I'll probably have to spank you."

"No worries. Come on," Jade said, pushing him away from her. "Go inside and quit stalling."

"I like stalling." He pulled her back. "Let's get in my truck and make a baby."

She gazed up at him. "No strings attached?"

He kissed her. "Of course there'll be strings attached. Don't be weird."

She pulled back to gaze up at him. "Excuse me? I'm the weird one? And you're what?"

"Not weird." He allowed himself to taste the sweet heaven of her lips again. It was really the only way to keep her quiet. Anyway, kissing her had the knock-on effect of getting that freight train roaring inside his head again, which was awesome, because it really did run off the ghosts and the past he didn't want to examine closely. Or at all.

"Listen," Jade said, jerking away from him, taking a few deep breaths. "I'm just in this for a baby."

He laughed. "You're such a fibber. You have a seriously hot thing going for me, Jade Harper."

She sniffed. "Wouldn't you like to think that?"

"I do think that." He glanced at the star-speckled sky, delighted to have gotten under her skin. She simply didn't want to admit that she was crazy about him. But she was here with him now, wasn't she?

"Whenever I kiss you," Ty said, "my mind goes totally blank. All I can think about is you, and your mouth, and that body of yours."

She stared at him. "You're a little hot yourself. A little."

He laughed out loud, picked her up, tossed her over his shoulder. Carried her up the porch steps over her protests, slapped her rump once just to let her know he was the boss and that everything was going his way tonight, stuck his key in the lock and pushed the door open.

The warm fragrance of his father's pipe hit him, even though the man had been gone a few years. A combination of cherrywood and tobacco, the aroma brought the feeling of home rushing over Ty. He set Jade gently on her feet as he took in the single lamp that burned in the kitchen. The wood floors gleamed with polish, and not a speck of dust marred any of the furniture. If he listened hard, he could hear the sound of his father's big boots coming down the stairs. Ty's heart hammered; he held his breath, waiting for something that wasn't going to happen.

Those big arms weren't waiting anymore to scoop up the little boy when he came rushing in the door from school, anxious to see his father. "Damn," Ty muttered.

Jade stood very still beside him, not intruding on his memories. After a moment, she very gently inserted her hand into his, and he tightened his grip, grateful for the contact.

He took a deep breath, walked into the kitchen. Cosette had had a new refrigerator put in, a big silver affair that could hold an army's worth of food. He smiled, liking the way it looked in the big kitchen. Many a meal had been consumed here, the three of them at the round table with four wooden chairs, in the nook window overlooking the garden, and past that, the fields. "Damn," he said again, and Jade pressed up against his side, supporting him.

He went out of the kitchen, walked up the stairs, Jade at his side. Three bedrooms at the top led from the central hall. Ty pushed open the door to his room, his heart thudding.

The bedroom took up the entire east side of the upstairs. His toys and childhood memorabilia were in their right places, his trophies stacked on the shelves. Nothing had been moved.

"It's like a time capsule," Jade said. "As if you never left."

But he had. And he wouldn't have come back except that he wanted to say goodbye to the small town that had been his home. He'd had this grand dream that he could save the community, or weight the scales more in the favor of good.

Tonight's fight had shown how difficult that was going to be.

"Listen, we probably ought to go." Ty took a deep breath. "Thanks for coming out with me."

She put her hand in his. "Your parents loved you a lot, Ty. You know that. Terence never thought of you as his adopted son. You were the son of his heart."

"I know." He'd been a father in every way. Which made the fact that Ty hadn't been around for him much a pretty rotten guilt trip. "Hey, Jade."

"Yeah?" She looked at him with those big green eyes, and he felt himself falling in.

"About your situation." He gestured with a hand, feeling frustrated, not sure how to bring up such a delicate topic. "I know we were kidding around earlier about your, um, ovary—"

"It's okay," she said quickly, trying to ward him off. "It was a while ago."

He scraped a hand through his short hair, a military-ready cut that reminded him he had a future he was heading to in a few brief days. "I missed a lot of things, not being around. But I want you to know that—" he took a deep breath "—I'm sorry for whatever you went through. I know it wasn't easy."

"I had a cyst that burst." She looked sad. "It wasn't much fun, I'll admit. Pretty horrible, actually."

"I'm so sorry." He felt pain in his chest, physical pain, that she'd suffered in a way he could never imagine, not only physically but psychologically. He knew the emotional trauma was there, or she wouldn't have brought up her wild plan of trying to get pregnant. Which was feeling less wild all the time, and somehow strangely like a really good idea.

A clear sign it was time to leave. "Hey," he said, pulling her close, "let's blow this joint."

She relaxed against him just for a moment. "Good idea."

There was too much heat searing him. He was glad she wanted to leave as much as he did. Being alone with her wasn't his best idea—there weren't any barriers here. Nothing to keep him from making the huge mistake of getting entangled where he definitely wanted most to be tangled up.

They went down the stairs together, side by side, not speaking. Suddenly Jade slipped, and he reached to grab her, and they fell the last few steps into the foyer.

"Are you all right?" He got up, went to inspect her.

She gazed up at him with those incredible eyes, looking stunned.

"I'm fine. I think."

"Let me help you to the sofa."

"Not yet. Let me lie here a second and gather my wits."

He wasn't sure his wits could ever be gathered if she'd gotten injured because of him. "Are you hurt?"

"I'm trying to figure that out. Don't look, but I'm going to do an indelicate kind of roll to my side, get up kind of thing."

"Whatever works for you. Let me know how I can help."

His heart was racing way too hard. He was pretty certain she was blinking back tears as she got to her knees, thankfully making it to the large, soft rug that graced the living area.

"I'm just going to lie here on this comfy rug for a few moments," Jade told him. "Please stop looking like that. You're scaring me."

"Do you want me to call someone? A doctor?"

"I'm fine. I think I knocked the breath clean out of me and stunned myself. I see a few spots when I try to get up. I'll be fine in a second."

He glanced back at the stairwell. "Luckily, it was only two or three steps. I'm sorry I didn't catch you."

"My foot slipped right out from under me. I can't imagine why."

She was wearing boots; maybe she'd caught a slick spot on the uncarpeted stairs. "Let me help you move to a sofa."

"Okay. Thanks."

He helped her to a sitting position. "How's that?"

"Fine so far," Jade said.

"Great. Put your arm around my neck, and—" Dear God, he could smell perfume and see just a bit of cleavage beneath her red sweater. Thankfully, she'd been wearing a puffy coat or she might have really hurt herself. Ty tried not to think about how warm and soft she was, and he was almost succeeding when he realized that holding Jade this close, her arm wrapped around him so trustingly, had given him an erection of epic proportions.

This was not good.

He was crazy about this woman. And she wasn't exactly pushing him away. In fact, if he didn't know better, he'd think she might have just snuggled a little closer against his chest, in the opening his sheepskin jacket provided. Close enough to feel his heart beating, which was thumping as hard as a drum in a parade.

The front door opened, and Cosette peered in at them, her mouth opening a little in surprise.

"Ty!" she exclaimed.

"Hi, Cosette." He noticed Jade trying to wriggle away from him, realized a strand of the red hair he adored was caught on one of his jacket buttons, making escape impossible.

"I saw the lights on," Cosette said, sounding breathless and worried. "I was on my way home. I wasn't expecting you to be here, and I only ever leave the kitchen lamp on. The door was open—"

"Cosette, it's fine. I'm glad you're here." He really was—he desperately needed separation from Jade in more ways than one. "Can you help me with Jade?"

"Of course! What's wrong?"

"I tumbled down the stairs," Jade said, "although I

don't know if you can call three steps a tumble. And now I'm caught in Ty's jacket."

"I can see." Cosette nodded and closed the door, but didn't do anything to help release her from the proximity of Ty's chest. If anything, she seemed completely happy for Jade to remain in his arms, and Ty reminded himself that she was named Madame Matchmaker for the exact reason that she had a matchmaking business, and she was, in fact, damn fine at it.

Too good, in fact, as testified by the matchmaking ledger she kept in her office.

"Cosette, Jade's hair is caught in my coat," he reminded her. "Can you help her? Because I can't see it, obviously." Not with the way Jade was crushed up against his chest. He was afraid to move her lest he pull her hair and hurt her.

"I feel like we need a photo of this moment," Cosette said, pulling out her phone and snapping a quick picture. "There," she said, pleased. "We'll have something for the memory books. We do love our memory books in Bridesmaids Creek."

His jaw dropped, and yet he shouldn't be the least bit surprised by anything the inhabitants of BC did. "Cosette, a little help, please? Jade is hurt and I want to get her to the sofa."

"Yes, please," Jade said, sounding very tired suddenly.

It scared the hell out of him. She was always so perky. He began to worry about a concussion, which was stupid, because he was pretty certain she hadn't hit her head. But maybe he hadn't noticed. His heart started that uncertain hammering again, reminding him that this woman meant so much to him he couldn't bear for anything to happen to her. He should have protected her. How could a man feel like a competent protector when he let her fall down a staircase?

"Have you had the stairs polished recently?" he asked Cosette, as she peered at the hank of Jade's hair snagged on his button.

"No," she murmured. "They're in fine condition. Your father made those stairs with his own hands, remember. We're going to have to cut this, I'm afraid, Jade. Your hair got caught in the buckle."

"I guess it's my just deserts for cutting Daisy's hair," Jade said.

"No. It's not any dessert." Ty wished he could shrug out of his jacket so he could see how to help, but if anybody could figure out how to disentangle them, it was Cosette.

"Where are your scissors?" she asked. "Never mind. They're in a kitchen drawer."

He was happy to hear it, because he hadn't lived here in so many years that he didn't even know if a pair of scissors remained. Cosette beetled off, and Ty wrapped his arms tight around Jade.

"Let me get you over to the sofa."

"I'm fine. I just tried to knock myself silly, is all."

"That would be a very hard thing to do, since you're one of the smartest women I've ever met." He helped her to the sofa, and they sat down together.

"This is so awkward," Jade whispered. "Cosette is going to tell everyone about this."

"Hell, yes, she is. She has the photo to show. Luckily for us, it's pretty tame stuff." If she'd opened the door and found him kissing the daylights out of Jade, as he wanted to be doing—now that would have been awkward.

He wished he had been kissing Jade. Ty felt that a golden opportunity had slipped away from him.

Cosette returned, peering at him, her big eyes illuminated by her pink-cast hair. "Don't look."

"Why not?"

"Because I don't want you being a big baby about it," she said. "It's just hair. It'll grow back. By the time you make it back to BC the next time, you'll never be able to tell the difference."

"Very funny," he said, noting her dig about his frequent absences. "Just do it, already." If she didn't get Jade away from him, get the sweet scent of her shampoo and body away from him immediately, he wasn't going to be able to think straight for a month. He was already pretty much lost in the fantasy of kissing her—and that wasn't going anywhere very fast.

"There!" Cosette exclaimed, examining her handiwork as Jade pulled away, rubbing her head. "Free as a bird!"

"Thank you, Cosette," Jade said.

"Ah, well, curly red hair has its dangers. And now I must be off!" The older woman wound her scarf tighter around her neck, beamed at the two of them. "Lock up tight, Ty."

"I will."

She went to the front door, hesitating as she watched him settle Jade on the sofa.

"It's good to see you back here in the old place, Ty," Cosette said. "Good night, you two."

She went out, locking the door behind her.

Jade looked up at him. "Sorry about that."

"Sorry for what?" He couldn't imagine what she had to be sorry about.

"For—I don't know. Making an ass of myself."

He couldn't imagine any woman ever being less of an ass than Jade. "You'll be happy to know that you won't miss this little bit of hair."

"Right. Because it's right in the front." Jade sighed. "It's karma for what I did to Daisy."

"Nonsense. And you look totally hot with short hair. That angled look is really wickedly hot." He wanted desperately to kiss her, so desperately that he decided to busy himself inspecting the staircase—anything to stay away from her until she felt steady enough to leave.

The stairs had been barely used in all the years he'd been gone. Cosette hadn't had them polished. Possibly Jade had simply had a clumsy moment, but she wasn't a clumsy woman. He peered at the spot where she'd slipped, realizing there was a crack in the stairs. A slight crack only an eighth of an inch wide, separating the stair board from the box underneath.

That would have to be repaired. Clearly, she'd somehow caught her heel on the uneven step and slipped. He moved his fingers along the edges to see if he could push them back together until it could be properly repaired. It wouldn't do to have Cosette taking a tumble.

The stair glided back into place as easy as a jigsaw puzzle piece locking into its correct match. He tugged at it to test the stability, and the wood moved toward him again. "This is definitely not secure," he told Jade.

She came to stand beside him. "Maybe the house has shifted, loosening the boards."

"Maybe." Anything could happen, but his father had been a fine carpenter. He'd even built the balustrade and carved the stair rail, a beautiful, polished mahogany work of art that had stood the test of time. Ty tugged at the board once more, determined now to pull it apart so that Cosette wouldn't step on it until it could be fixed.

The wood piece completely separated from the stair, and though he expected to find nothing at all underneath, a metal box came into view.

"Yikes," Jade said. "This place *is* like a time capsule."

A strange sensation came over Ty, a sense that something wasn't right. Nobody hid gray metal boxes in stairwells unless they didn't want them found.

No one could have put this here but his father.

"Are you going to open it?" Jade asked.

"I don't think so," Ty said softly. "I think I'm going to close up this house and get the hell out of Dodge." While he still could. Before the tendrils of BC could pull him any deeper.

She put a hand on his shoulder. "Maybe that's a good idea."

"You think so?" Nothing good came of opening hidden boxes and releasing another person's ghosts.

"Yeah. Navy SEAL advice, remember? Get your affairs in order, and leave everything—"

"Yeah. You're right." He pushed the wood piece back over the box, shoving it into place again. The hole disappeared like magic.

Before he left town, he was going to buy some serious, ass-binding wood glue to seal this off. Whatever it took, that box wasn't going to see the light of day again.

"I guess it could always be gold," Jade said. "Buried treasure."

"I'm not much for believing in fairy tales." Besides which, his father had been an assiduous businessman.

Everything had been noted down to the penny; the records and accounts had been easy to find and settle after his death. If he'd left gold, money or valuables in a safe somewhere, he would have marked that in his business records. There'd only been one safe deposit box, and then an old iron safe in the basement that would take a crane to move. Ty had known about those. But his father had built the stairs, and whatever he'd secured away there he hadn't wanted to ever be found.

Which meant nothing good was in this box. "Let's get out of here."

Jade kissed Ty when he stood up.

"What was that for?"

"Because I think you're brave."

He wasn't brave. Not at all.

But he wasn't about to admit it. He pulled her into his arms instead, reigniting the passion they'd shared earlier, taking the gentle kiss she'd just given him into the inferno he wanted—needed—right now.

The one thing he had in his life that was secure and sane was this crazy redhead who drove him out of his mind. He'd taken too long to admit it to himself, but he was going to miss the hell out of her.

His affairs were not in order, not by a long shot.

"Either we leave now or I'm going to lose the battle between my conscience and my—"

She stopped his words with a kiss. "Lose it, already. I've waited way too long for you to get over that schoolboy conscience of yours."

Well, hellfire. There it was, the invitation a man could not pass up. He couldn't, not when kissing Jade was the best thing that had happened to him in a long time. He wanted to spend hours losing himself in her, thinking about nothing but her beautiful body and her sassy mouth and the way she made him grin.

He carried her up the stairs to his old room, laid her gently on the bed, turned on a lamp.

She stared up at him, her eyes huge in her pale face, the slight freckles standing out. He had never seen anything more beautiful, never desired anyone the way he did her. She pulled off the red sweater, revealing a white lacy bra with a tiny pink bow in the center, and something about that trusting, inviting gesture was so sexy that Ty knew in that moment that Jade Harper had completely, irrevocably stolen his heart, in spite of his best efforts to keep his heart selfishly to himself.

"You know what we're doing here," Jade said, and Ty halted in the act of diving in and ripping her clothes six ways from Sunday.

"Making love?"

"Avoiding the buried box."

He nodded, his full-on erection urging him to get on with the diving in he so desperately wanted to do. Still, if Jade was having a change of heart, he'd tell his poor, tortured body and soul that there'd be no diving of any kind today, unless it wanted to go for a really long, cold swim in Bridesmaids Creek. "Probably. Are you okay with that?"

"I'm *so* okay with that." Jade undid his belt buckle and looked up at him. "Whatever excuse works is fine by me."

There was sweet satin and lace waiting for him, and a redhead who wanted him. There might never be this much willing paradise in his life again.

He dived in.

Chapter Nine

The hours of holding Jade in his arms could never be replaced by anything better—never. Ty felt as if he'd died and gone to heaven, on rocket propulsion and faster than angels flew. As she lay on his chest, he stroked her skin, trying to figure out what he was going to do now.

He had to do something.

"I'd better go," Jade said. "It's almost morning."

He didn't want her to go. They'd spent hours making mind-blowing love, hardly speaking, letting their bodies do the talking. "I can't let you."

She laughed softly. "I never thought I'd hear those words from the mouth of such a rolling stone."

"I'm not kidding." He wasn't. His life had changed in ways he couldn't have imagined. You just didn't make love to a woman and then go off as if it hadn't mattered—at least not if you'd finally caught the woman of your dreams and something very, very close to love had smacked you right upside the head, bringing you to a very clear realization of how wonderful your future could be if you could keep that woman of your wild and crazy dreams.

She rolled up on his chest to gaze down at him. "It's

not like I haven't always been here in BC. You know where to find me."

"Yeah. So does Sam."

She smiled sexily at Ty. "You brought those fine hunks to town."

He hadn't meant for one of them to make Jade fall in love with him. And as Jade appeared to be on something of a baby-making mission, it was a concern that weighed on Ty. "Hunks, huh?"

She raised a brow, kissed him. "Just a little."

He could tell she was teasing him and enjoying it, but the thing was, he had this really strong urge to put a name on whatever it was they had between them. "I don't like Sam," he said with a growl.

Jade laughed. "You think the world of Sam. Anyway," she said, kissing him again, making him think about the fact that he should be kissing her, and in the most strategic places possible. "Sam isn't a stayer."

"A stayer?"

"Mmm-hmm. Haven't you noticed? Sam isn't going to be your success story. You're far more likely to settle down than Sam. And Frog and Toad are guaranteed."

Frog and Toad? Ty might have laughed if he wasn't so worried. "Frog and Squint are good guys. Sam is, too," he admitted grudgingly. "How do you know he isn't going to settle?"

"He's just along for the ride."

"You spent enough time with him to figure that out?" Ty asked, unable to help himself from sounding like a jealous schmuck.

"He just doesn't have any desire to stay in one place, Ty. Sort of like you."

She pressed gentle kisses on his chest, tantalizing him.

"So what if we made a baby?" he asked.

The kisses stopped. "You're good, handsome, but I really don't think you're so good that a couple of nights—"

"I'm trying really hard. And I have a confession to make."

"Do confess." She cocked her head, waiting.

"I'd like to spend the rest of time before I leave dedicating myself to that goal."

She looked at him for a long time. "I have a confession to make myself."

His heart hitched. He hoped like hell she wasn't going to tell him that this was a one-shot deal. "Your turn."

"I'm on the same drug that Mackenzie was on when she got pregnant. It's to help women conceive when it's been difficult for them to do so."

"Why were you already on it?" He refused to think she might have been playing up to Sam for the very purpose of getting that baby she wanted.

"The day you came home, I went and talked to the doctor."

His jaw literally sagged. "You never once let on that you wanted to date me. Or even be more than friends."

She wrinkled her nose. "It's not the kind of thing a woman just blurts out to a man. Although I did mention to you tonight that—"

He sat up. "Yeah, you mentioned it tonight, a handful of days before I'm leaving, and simply to keep me from jumping into a fight!"

She shrugged, which made her very tempting breasts jiggle a little. He was utterly fascinated—but forced himself back to the conversation. "It took me a while to get my courage up. The fight sort of pushed me to the moment."

"I'm glad something did," he groused. He hated to think he might have gone off and never known that this woman had sexy plans for him. "Holy crap."

"Yeah."

"So there's really a chance we could make a baby, since you're on this turbo-ovary-booster stuff."

She smiled. "It worked for Mackenzie."

He could be a dad. Holy, holy crap.

"But I'm pretty sure it's not the right time of the month," Jade said.

His world crashed. "How do you know? Doesn't the medicine override all that?"

She laughed. "I'm afraid not."

"Hell."

"It's okay."

No, it really wasn't. He didn't have enough time to give this his best shot. And something inside him really, really wanted to do just that. "So you wanna get married?"

"No." She laughed again and got out of the bed. "You're going to do your SEAL thing. Don't try to use me to get out of it."

Use her, hellfire. He wanted to have her for the rest of his time here. He wanted everything she wanted to give him and then some. "But if I did hit the target, you'd marry me, right?"

She reached for her panties, clearly getting ready to bolt. "You're going into the navy. That's all you ever talked about. Let's focus on that goal."

"I just don't want to come home to find you married," he grumbled, knowing he was being totally unreasonable. He didn't like the way she'd skirted the issue of marriage, either. It hadn't been much of a proposal, as proposals went—more something that had flown unbidden out of his mouth. But she hadn't so much as blinked or smiled when he'd said it, and from that alone he discerned a decided lack of enthusiasm on her part.

He supposed she didn't have much to get excited about, since he really had nothing to offer her. She was right. He was leaving, and there was absolutely no knowing when he'd be back.

"I'm not done with you." He grabbed her, tugging her back into bed with him, encircling her with his arms and holding her against his chest. Anything to keep her with him just a little while longer.

"I have to leave."

She didn't sound all that convinced. Ty figured he knew what a woman sounded like when she was ready to hit the door, and Jade made no move to leave his arms, either. He nuzzled her neck, sighed against the soft skin. Felt himself get hard, and stroked a hand across her nipples, which perked up instantly. She was fitted against him in such a nice, comfortable spoon fashion, and he moved into place easily behind her, finding the soft sweetness he craved, sliding inside her as if they'd never been apart. Didn't belong apart. She moaned with pleasure, tucking herself closer against him, and Ty's every muscle tightened with desire he couldn't control. Something about her drove him completely out of his mind. Jade was the only woman who made him this insanely hungry. He teased her nipples, and when she gasped, rocking against him urgently, he slid a hand between her legs, stroking her, letting his fingers glide against her softness, taking his time bringing her to pleasure until she was gasping his name, begging him for release.

Still he gently kissed her neck, taking his time before sweeping her over the edge, enjoying her heat and her desire for him.

"Ty," she said, her voice an urgent plea.

He knew what she wanted. He could give it to her—he would. But he wanted her hovering with him at the edge of pleasure as long as possible, wanted her in his arms feeling this magic as long as he could keep her.

She tightened up on him, and he steeled himself, but between her soft words asking him to release her, and the wild tension of her rocking against him, Ty knew he couldn't last much longer. Taking a gentle bite of her shoulder, keeping her as close to him as he possibly could, he thrust into her as he teased her with his fingers until he could feel the soft, slick folds all around him tense, waiting. He tweaked her gently, burying himself deep inside her, and was rewarded by his name on her lips again as she gasped and cried out.

Then he allowed himself his own release into her welcoming body, his every muscle shuddering, his arms holding her for all he was worth.

This was what he wanted.

This was his new plan.

He didn't know how it could work out. It seemed impossible.

But if there was any way on God's green earth he could keep Jade for his own, he intended to do it.

JADE HAD TY take her home just before the sun came up. After the excitement last night with the fighting, and then somehow them ending up in bed together, everything had changed. Jade barely knew what to think. She slipped quickly from his truck before the moment could get awkward between them. If it never happened again, she wanted to remember last night just the way it had been—spontaneous and somehow magical.

She went inside her house, headed upstairs for a hot shower and a change of clothes before she went to find Betty.

Her mother looked up, smiling brightly, as she made it into the kitchen. "Good morning! There's coffee and I have a cake fresh out of the oven."

"It smells fabulous." Jade realized she was ravenous as she got a cup of coffee and slid onto a bar stool. "Thanks, Mom."

"Busy day ahead." Betty pulled out some eggs. "Thanks for all the help last night."

"Mom, I don't want you to do everything yourself. You can't run the ice-cream shop and do the treat stand at the Haunted H." Jade sighed with appreciation as her mother put a fresh-baked slice of cinnamon cake in front of her. "I can run the stand at night myself."

"I look at this two ways," Betty said, whipping the eggs in a bowl with some milk and other ingredients. "One, we're lucky to have the extra income the Haunted H is bringing in, and with the Donovans being totally against it, we have to make hay while the sun shines, because who knows how long it'll last. Two, I have help at the ice-cream shop. It's not that much work to run the stand, too."

Jade barely realized she'd wolfed down the entire piece of cake. "I was starving."

"You were out late," Betty observed mildly. "Probably didn't have dinner."

Jade sipped her coffee. "I don't know what I'm doing, Mom."

Betty didn't stop stirring, didn't glance up. "Does it matter?"

And that was her mother's subtle way of saying that she shouldn't overthink the situation with Ty, which had just taken a major complication turn. "You're right."

"Anyway," Betty said, "Cosette called me last night."

Jade looked at her mother. "I'm fine. I just fell down a couple of stairs."

Betty glanced up. "You fell down stairs?"

"Cosette didn't tell you?"

"My word, no. She called to tell me that Robert Donovan is continuing to put the squeeze on Phillipe. I don't think Mssr. Unmatchmaker's going to be able to hold out. And I think the divorce is going ahead, unfortunately. Too many financial issues, with Donovan pulling the strings." She looked puzzled. "How would Cosette have known you fell down some stairs?"

"Never mind. Long story." Maybe Cosette hadn't gone into full gossip mode as soon as she'd left Ty's place. Anyway, it didn't matter. Jade supposed she didn't care if people knew she'd gone out to Ty's place—even if folks would be a little surprised that he'd finally darkened that door after so many years. She certainly had been.

Strangely, it had felt so much like he'd come home. She'd felt him relaxing, unbending.

Until they'd unearthed the metal box. He hadn't said another word about that during the night, and she didn't figure he would. "I don't understand why Phillipe and Cosette's little matchmaking business is the immediate target of Mr. Donovan's evil plans."

"They're in the center of the block in town. If he can take that, he'll have more leverage with the other businesses." Betty put steaming eggs on a pretty blue plate in front of her. "Cosette is just devastated."

Jade's phone buzzed in the back pocket of her jeans. "This is delicious, Mom. I should be making you breakfast, though."

"Nonsense."

Jade pulled out her phone, smiling when she saw the message from Ty: Come back tonight—I have plans for you.

She texted back Plans?

Just dinner, beautiful. Don't be greedy.

She laughed. He did have high opinions of himself.

"Ah, young love," Betty said with a happy sigh.

Jade blinked. "I'm not in love, Mom. We're not in love."

"Ty and you, you mean."

Jade realized she had no secrets from her mother. "Yes." She texted back I'll bring dessert. Going to the Haunted H tonight?

Wouldn't miss it.

She put her phone away, her body already glowing with the secret knowledge of what she knew would happen tonight. "What do you think it would take to get Robert Donovan off our necks forever?"

"If I knew that," Betty said, sitting down with her own piece of cake and a cup of hot coffee, "I'd be blabbing it all over town."

"I feel sorry for Cosette and Phillipe." Jade lost her appetite. Cosette was just about the nicest person in Bridesmaids Creek. In fact, there was no better place to have grown up than BC. Everybody helped look out for each other. Jade had never been tempted to leave— not like Ty had wanted so badly to do.

She completely understood his reasons. "I think I'm going to spend some time with Ty until he has to go."

"That's nice, dear." Betty had her head buried in the Bridesmaids Creek newspaper now, looking for gossip items. "Try to keep him out of any more fighting until he leaves, is my advice. He needs all his strength for BUD/S."

Everybody supported Ty in his dream. Any time a BC son or daughter made something of themselves, the town celebrated, feeling a part of that success. Town pride was built in from birth. "I know. Thanks, Mom." Jade got up, took her dishes to the sink. "I'm going to clean the kitchen, then I'll run the stand tonight. Will you promise me to stay home and relax?"

Betty glanced up from the paper. "Why wouldn't I want to be where all the action is?" She laughed, shook her head. "Jade Harper, just because you're spending time with a hot man does not mean I'm ready to suddenly put on my slippers and sit in front of the TV. You couldn't keep me from the fun!"

Jade smiled fondly and shook her head, then began putting a few things away so Betty wouldn't have to. She'd gotten a lot accomplished when she heard the back door open.

"Hello!" a man's voice yelled into the house, like he'd done a thousand times before.

"In here, Ty!" Jade called, irrationally pleased that he'd shown up so soon.

He walked into the kitchen and Jade smiled. "Just like old times. You must have smelled the cinnamon cake a mile away."

He was so big and handsome—so sexy she could hardly stand it. All she could think of was the magic his hands worked on her, and his mouth, and his body against hers.

A flush of desire stole over her.

"No cake today, thanks." He kissed her mom on the cheek. "Do you mind if I steal your daughter for a moment?"

"Steal away." Betty waved her hand. "Do you want the kitchen?"

His gaze hitched to Jade's. "Can we chat outside, Jade?"

This was odd. He never passed up Betty's cake or pie. She looked him over, hearing an urgent tone in his voice. He wore jeans, a freshly pressed long-sleeved shirt, his sheepskin jacket—and a really serious expression. A shiver of concern ran over her, and maybe even a splash of premonition that she wasn't going to like whatever he'd come to say.

Chapter Ten

Jade walked outside with Ty, catching his serious mood like a virus. Lighthearted, daredevil-with-a-grin Ty—when was he ever this dark and quiet?

"What's going on?" she asked, anxious to get whatever it was out in the open.

He took a deep breath as they reached his truck, and leaned against the door. As if he meant to drive off at any second. Jade's heart rate kicked up.

"I have to leave today."

She hesitated. "Didn't we just text about getting together tonight?"

He nodded, his gaze dark and focused. "Those were the plans. The weather forecast is ugly, and flights are already being canceled around the U.S."

"I saw that on the news," she murmured, her heart sinking.

"I can't risk not showing up to BUD/S on time."

"No. Not at all." There would be no second chance, and being late wasn't an option. "You're absolutely right to go." Her heart felt as if it was shattering. She'd caught the weather report on the edge of her subconscious, barely paying attention to it, wrapped in the happy glow of the wonder of spending time in Ty's arms. "It's a wise decision to get ahead of flight cancelations. This winter has been busy with storms."

She took a deep breath, unable to say any more. The last thing she wanted was to make him feel guilty that he had to leave, when he was doing the exact thing she knew he needed to do, and which she wanted him to do.

"I want you to do something for me. It's a lot to ask." He took a deep breath, pulled her up against him.

"What do you need me to do?"

"I'll understand if you can't make the commitment. It's a huge favor."

She looked up into his eyes. "Okay."

"I want you to take over Cosette's job of watching the house. I don't know when I'll be back, and she's done it for me for years, but I'd feel better knowing you were in charge."

Jade nodded, understanding. He was trying to get his affairs in order, which underlined the finality of his imminent departure. She swallowed hard, not about to dim his leaving with news that Cosette and Phillipe's marriage appeared to be pretty much on the rocks. "It's fine. I can do it. It's probably for the best. Cosette's so busy these days."

His arms wrapped around her more tightly. "No one's busier than you are, lady. But you're special to me, you know that. And I keep thinking about that loose step, and Cosette stepping on it—"

"It's no problem. Take that off your plate of worries."

He kissed her forehead. "Here's the thing. I have a bigger favor to ask."

"Go on." At this point, she was going to say yes to whatever he mentioned. The best way to have him leave

with no worries in his rearview mirror was to do whatever she could to help.

"About the box…"

She watched him carefully. "Did you open it?"

"Hell, no. As I said, I knew all of Dad's business affairs. There's no hidden gold or something fantastic in
that box. Whatever it is, he meant to keep it hidden. I
have no desire to open Pandora's box. Not now."

"It can wait until you get back." She had a suspicion
he was right about leaving whatever it was buried.

"I've had a will drawn up," Ty said. "You're the sole
executor and beneficiary of my estate, should anything
happen to me."

Her mouth dropped open. "Why?"

"Who else is there?" He kissed her gently on the lips.
"And I would have no peace of mind whatsoever if that
supercharged ovary of yours decided it had bingoed."

She was stunned. Couldn't say anything. "Ty, you're
going to be fine. Nothing's going to happen."

"All affairs have to be in order."

She knew that. On one level it made total sense. On
the other hand, it forced her to realize that what he was
doing was very dangerous—and more so in the future,
if he was accepted into the SEALs.

Of course he would be. He'd worked his ass off to
realize his dream.

"All right," she murmured, not happily.

"You'll write me if you're pregnant? I'd be the world's
worst dad not to be here—"

"I'm not pregnant," she said. "I told you, I don't even
think I'm in the right time of my cycle."

"Damn." He looked a bit crestfallen, though he
smiled. "I really worked hard at that."

She laughed. "I noticed. It was wonderful."

He kissed her long and sweetly, drawing a sigh from her when he finally pulled away to look at her.

"Which brings us back to the box," he said.

She waited.

"I want you to open it after I'm gone."

A gasp flew from her before she could stop it. "I don't—"

"Hear me out." He cut off her words, holding her protectively in his arms. "You're the only person I trust with whatever's in there. Take care of what needs taking care of, in regards to the contents. I just don't want to know whatever secret Dad might have been keeping. I hope you understand."

"I do," she murmured. "I really do. I'm not comfortable with it, but I do."

"It's a huge favor, like I said. But I really want to leave with a clear head, and no BC drama hanging on to me."

"It's the least I can do." Jade took a deep breath. "You realize it's probably nothing other than…I don't know, maybe some important papers."

"Those were all in the vault. Anyway, here's the thing," Ty continued, obviously not caring to linger on whatever secrets his father might have left behind. "After you go through the contents, I want you to seal the step back up. I've left the materials to do that. I figure you know how to work with wood, since you help your mother set up the stand at the haunted house."

"It's no problem." She was actually pretty handy at repairing lots of things. Small-business owners learned how to do things for themselves. "I can take care of it."

He kissed her one last time, his lips lingering over

hers. "This isn't how I wanted to say goodbye. I had planned for something more romantic, not dumping all my final requests on you."

"It's fine." She was still stunned that he was leaving so quickly. It felt as if part of her was being ripped away.

"I've told Cosette she's off the case. Here are the keys." Ty handed Jade financial documents and a key ring. "Believe me, I'd rather be giving you a different kind of ring, Jade."

Her gaze flew to his. "I think we both know that's not realistic."

After a long moment, he nodded. "I guess not."

"Go," she said, feeling on the verge of tears she didn't want to cry in front of him. "Be the best damn SEAL the navy ever trained."

He smiled, his mouth a little crooked. "You always believed in my dream."

"Of course I do. If Frog and Squint and Sam can be SEALs, you ought to really make BC proud."

He grinned. "Your faith is inspiring."

"I just know you. You've never set a goal you didn't achieve, Ty."

He looked at her. "I never really thought of myself that way, but I guess you're right."

"Of course I'm right." She kissed him one last time. "Please hit the road." The papers and key ring felt heavy in her hands. She wanted to drop them and throw her arms around his neck, beg him not to leave, at least not so quickly.

But he had to.

"You mean a lot to me, Jade Harper."

She smiled bravely. "And you mean a lot to me. You'll mean even more with a Trident."

"I don't know when I'll be back."

"You don't know if you'll ever be back," she said. "And that's exactly the way it should be. You haven't dreamed this dream for so long to be pulled back to Bridesmaids Creek, Ty. The only reason you came home was to save us. In lieu of a going-away party from BC, I freely tell you to get your ass in that truck and don't look in the rearview mirror. Nothing ever changes here. We're a mirage in time."

"A town of carnies," he said. "Everybody selling their shtick and the BC legend."

"That's right. Now go sell yours."

Ty looked at her for a long time. "I would have swum the creek for you. Even done the Best Man's Fork run. And that's something I've never said to anyone."

"Our BC legends are pretty entangling. Be careful what you say." She smiled, but he didn't return it, his gaze serious. Her heart ached, but he had to go. He'd always feel he'd fallen short of his goal and his dreams if he didn't. A few hours of wonderful lovemaking shouldn't change everything he'd planned for. "Now go, cowboy."

He nodded, got in the truck. "But if there should be a baby—"

"There isn't. Goodbye." She kissed him on the mouth through the window opening, smiled as big as she could, selling shtick as hard as she could. "Good luck."

"Thanks."

He looked at her for a long moment, his eyes serious and dark, then started the engine. He drove away, his truck headed down the road toward the Hanging H, where he'd say his goodbyes to his buddies. She imagined shouts and laughter, and assumed Sam would drive him to the airport. She wished Ty would have asked her to take him, knew that would have been a really bad idea. Airports were no place for goodbyes, not goodbyes that were forever.

She carried the papers and the house keys inside.

Her heart rode off with Ty.

Chapter Eleven

Eleven months later

"These little ladies don't look like their father," Sam observed, looking down into the bassinet where little Marie and Eve blinked their eyes like tiny dolls.

Jade shook her head. "Considering most of the town thinks they're yours, you better not say that too loudly."

He grinned. "Aw, I wouldn't mind if they were."

She raised a brow.

"I just mean I wouldn't mind having some kids," he said hurriedly. "But I'm sure not hitting on you, Jade."

She laughed. "I know."

Sam hung around a lot now that she'd had the girls, as did Frog and Squint. She'd never admitted that Ty was the father, not to a soul except Betty—and her mother would never give up her secret. Sam was just fishing, doing his usual trickster thing.

"I just want that to be clear," he continued, "because one day Ty is going to ride back into town, and I don't want him beating my head in if someone tells him I was flirting with his girl."

"I'm not Ty's girl." Jade swallowed hard. "Don't be silly."

"It's not a matter of silly. You're taking care of his house. Ty wouldn't let anyone take care of his homestead unless he trusted them and felt strongly about them."

"Sorry to blow up your theory," Jade said breezily, reaching into the bassinet to pick up Eve, "but you're aware that Cosette used to do this same job I'm doing? Keeping an eye on the Spurlock place?"

Sam shook his head. "I'm not buying the story you're selling, sister, but whatever." He scooped up Marie. "I do love babies. And these girls are sweet."

A little uneasy that he'd guess her secret, Jade wanted to get Sam's attention on a different topic. "Maybe you should consider running in the Best Man's Fork race."

"Maybe I shouldn't." Sam nuzzled the baby. "I think you may have done something unattractive in your diaper, little one, and yet somehow I can't find it entirely unattractive."

Jade laughed. "That's bad, Sam."

"I can change diapers faster than Houdini can disappear. I've had lots of experience." He did just that at the change table with impressive speed and efficiency.

"Are you sure you won't at least consider the Bridesmaids Creek swim? It's very, very lucky," Jade said. "Guaranteed to bring you a bride, if you win."

"Oh, I could win," Sam bragged, "but I don't want a bride. My goal is to be free and easy for the rest of my life."

"We have lots of pretty ladies around here." She looked up as she tested a bottle. "Anyway, Ty brought you here to find a wife. Aren't you stating that you have conflicting goals?"

"Look, it's easy. Squint and Frog want women. Justin didn't think he wanted one, but he got five. I think that's hilarious." Sam grinned. "Frog's trying to romance the socks off of Suz, much good may it do my brother in arms. And Squint's determined to tame the tornado known as Daisy. I figure everybody's settled and accounted for, and if I slip through Ty's net, that's fine. He'll just have to be happy with his success rate, and then get his own house in order." Sam glanced at Jade. "You still haven't told him, have you?"

"I'm not going to, and neither are you." She took a deep breath. "The time will be right one day, but it's not now. And you know it as well as I do."

"He was pretty proud when he wrote that he was now truly one of us," Sam said.

"And he took off for Afghanistan as fast as he could get sent. Or wherever he really went." There hadn't been a lot of news from Ty, and Jade felt a twinge about that. She'd stayed awake many nights during her pregnancy, wanting so badly to tell him, but not about to rock his world. "Anyway, what should I have done? Told him before he was even finished with BUD/S that he was going to be a father? You and I both know he would have come rushing back home." She swallowed hard, knowing it was true. Ty felt strongly about family, and the fact that he was adopted poured determination into his soul. He would have returned—and they would have had no future. You didn't take someone's long-held dream and dash it on the rocks, then expect that he wouldn't look back with some regret. Oh, Ty was too good of a man to be bitter or resentful—but it wouldn't be the same as it had been during that blissful time they'd shared in his house.

"I have to go do something." Jade had put this particular errand off long enough. "I'm going to call Mom over to watch the babies."

"I can do it," Sam said.

"You should be working." She went to find Betty, who'd staked out her place in the kitchen. "I need to run over to the…the Spurlock place real quick, Mom. Can you watch the girls?"

"Of course I can!" Flour flew as Betty put the lid on a canister. "Let me wash up."

She glanced over her shoulder at her daughter as she stood at the French sink. "I thought you were on the once-a-month schedule of going over there."

"I am." Jade covered the cookies her mother had baked with a paper towel, knowing they wouldn't be around long enough to bother putting them in a canister. "There's something I need to take care of."

"Suits me. I needed a baby break!" Betty sailed out of the kitchen, and Jade could hear her admonishing Sam to go find the cookies because he was looking too thin.

Sam wasn't too thin—but if he and the fellows didn't quit hanging around here so much, they were going to gain very un-SEAL-like pounds. Jade put on a scarf and coat to protect her against the cool wind—December was bringing much colder weather—and hurried to her truck.

Fifteen minutes later she was at Ty's, cautiously unlocking the door. As always, the house seemed welcoming and secure to her—but she never opened the door that her gaze didn't go straight to the stair step she had yet to repair.

She'd put off pulling out the metal box as long as she could. Today was the day, she vowed. The babies were two months old; Ty wasn't coming back. No one went into the house except her and Betty. Jade dropped in from time to time, checking over the place, turning on every tap to make sure everything was running properly, running a light rag over every surface to pick up dust. When she'd been ordered to bed for three months during her pregnancy—the doctor had been worried about her carrying the babies to term—Betty had come over in her place. Jade had told her mother that the third stair was loose, and not to step on it. Ty planned to repair his father's handiwork when he came home one day.

Betty had thought that sounded reasonable, and the subject never came up again. Jade had mostly put Ty's wishes concerning the box out of her mind. Part of her had hesitated because there was the tiniest chance he might come home—but that would mean he hadn't made it through BUD/S, and she definitely didn't want that.

It was really hard to think about opening a box Ty's father had left behind, but she understood why Ty didn't want to do it, why he was happier closing up the past for good. She'd promised herself that by the twins' two-month birthday, she was going to quit putting off the special mission Ty had entrusted her with.

She briefly considered repairing the step and not examining the contents of the box, but it was a small favor he'd asked, considering all he'd done for her. Anyway, it would take only a moment.

Jade tugged the step apart, finding the box undisturbed, though it still surprised her in some way to see it. The box's placement was so odd, nestled into the dark shelter of the stairs. Whatever was inside was something Sheriff Spurlock couldn't toss away, and yet didn't want Ty finding, a perfect hiding place from an active boy who might randomly see something his father didn't want him to see.

Yet maybe it was something good. Love letters, or a tiny statuette blessed for the house the sheriff had built.

Encouraged, Jade pulled the box out, and sat on the bottom step. Slowly she opened it, staring down at the pile of papers inside. On top of the stack lay an envelope with no writing on it. She picked it up, took a deep breath and pulled out the letter inside.

Dear Ty,

If you're reading this letter, I've probably gone to the big ranch in the sky. I left instructions with Phillipe LaFleur—Mssr. Unmatchmaker—that if you ever decided to sell the house—or if Robert Donovan managed to take over Bridesmaids Creek for good—that he was to give you a sealed letter I'd left in his possession. The letter gave you instructions on how to find this box, and I ask you in advance to forgive me for not telling you the truth in person. I never wanted to, could never see the reason to honor a man by ruining your life, which I think would have happened if you'd learned my secret during your formative years. If I had my way, this secret wouldn't ever make it to the light of day—certainly not until after Donovan's death.

But skeletons don't always stay buried, and the fact is, you are Robert Donovan's true son. Donovan's wife, Honoria, who was born and raised in BC, came home here and confided to my wife, Emily, during her pregnancy that Robert didn't know she was expecting, and that she planned to leave the state to have you, and give you up for adoption. Emily talked her into allowing us to adopt you, as long as we never, ever told Robert the truth.

As Emily couldn't have children, we jumped on the opportunity to have a child of our own, and Honoria was happy to know that her child was going to be living with us. We didn't know Robert that well then—he wasn't from here, and we figured our secret was safe. They were living at the time in Houston. It wasn't that she didn't want you, son. Honoria had realized she didn't love Robert, and she wanted no part of having a child with him. By then he'd already begun to show the seeds of the evil he'd later develop, and Honoria had quickly realized she didn't want to stay with him, wanted no ties with him. He would have never left her alone, anyway, if he'd known she was having his child.

Of course, you know this means that you're Daisy's older brother. You'll wonder how the Donovans ended up staying together, and even having a child together.

Honoria told Emily years later in confidence that upon her return from having you in Pennsylvania (we met her there and picked you up as soon as you came into the world), Robert professed his undying love for her and swore to change his ways. He'd missed her during her extended absence, fearing she had no intention of returning. Honoria decided to give her marriage one last chance, and Daisy was born a couple of years later. They moved here to BC for good when Daisy was about three years old. Secretly, I think Honoria was thrilled with the chance to keep an eye on you as you grew up. I think she also didn't realize that by then Robert had chosen BC as the perfect place to launch his empire, or she might never have returned here. I know their marriage wasn't a happy one after Daisy's birth, as Robert became hungrier and hungrier in his ambitions. Something about having a child of his own seemed to spur those ambitions. He was determined to create a kingdom for his name and his only child.

Jade stopped reading, stunned beyond words at the secrets spilling from the pages. It was almost too horrible to contemplate. She was fiercely glad Ty had never opened the box. She felt certain he would have never left BC, would have made it his mission to stay here and thwart his birth father at every turn of his evil steps.

A shudder ran over her that had nothing to do with the cool temperature at which she kept the house, or the gathering dark clouds outside, warning of a massive snow dump before the night was out.

She returned to the letter, her hands trembling a little.

Son, inside the box you'll find your birth certificate, as well as a gift from Honoria. The end of the story isn't a pleasant one. As you know, Daisy is straight from the DNA of her father, which you somehow escaped, thankfully. You brought your mother and me a lot of joy over the years, Ty. After Emily died I could sit in this house and think about the happy memories we had as a family. I can still hear your little footsteps thumping down the stairs. I can see your happy smile every night when I came home. I can see you running footballs into the end zone, and escorting the Homecoming queen. More than that, you were good to us, son. You were the miracle we would have never had in our lives. Forgive us, please, for keeping you to ourselves. You were the hope and the dream we never expected to have, and you were the son we'd always prayed for. You grew into a good man, and you made us proud. As far as Emily and I were concerned, you were ours, and the thing we loved the most.

I love you, son.

Dad

Tears jumped into Jade's eyes, streaming down as she put the letter back inside the envelope. She flipped through the other paperwork, but there was nothing else other than what Terence had mentioned, and a tiny box she assumed was the gift from his mother. Jade opened that quickly, wiping at her tears.

It was a small sterling Saint Michael medal, almost identical to the one Frog wore. Ty's full name was engraved on the back. Jade returned the medal to the velvet pouch, thinking that Ty would have liked such a gift. She closed the box, hesitated only a moment as she realized with dawning horror that Robert Donovan was the blood grandfather to her children, and Daisy the girls' aunt.

It was too much to contemplate right now. Jade crammed the box back into its secret nest and went to get the repair items Ty had left for her. She sealed the step back into place with wood glue, making sure it was tight and secure.

No one would ever know Sheriff Spurlock's secret. It would certainly never fall from her lips.

Satisfied with her handiwork, she put the toolbox away, then slipped on her coat, anxious to be away from the house. A promise was a promise, and she'd kept her promise to Ty. She felt immensely better now that she'd discharged her final duty—but her heart was heavy.

The door blew open on a gust of wind and icy puffs of cold. She gasped, staring into Ty's eyes as he filled the doorway, dark and forbidding and somehow not the Ty she remembered. A dark stranger gazed back at her, his face lean with hard planes, his body taut and muscle-packed.

"Ty!" Jade exclaimed. "You're home!"

He nodded, closed the door. "Yeah. I guess you could say that." He jerked his head toward the door. "I saw your truck. Hope I didn't scare you."

"No." She backed up a step. "Of course not."

She wasn't frightened, but her heart raced in spite of her words. The man she'd made love to no longer seemed to reside in his dark eyes. He didn't smile, didn't seem glad to see her.

If anything, he seemed remote.

"The roads are getting bad. You shouldn't be driving in the dark."

"No." She tightened her jacket, gulped a little nervously. "I should go."

He sniffed the air. "Do I smell glue? Paint?"

She shook her head. "I just cleaned the kitchen sink. You're probably smelling that."

He nodded, sighed tiredly. "Probably. Thanks for watching the house for me."

"It wasn't a problem at all," she said nervously, doing a little skitter around him to get to the door.

His hand shot out, grabbing her arm as she edged past. Her eyes caught on his gaze, her heart banging wildly inside her.

"I'm wiped," Ty said. "I've been on flights and in airports for the past three days, and I'm probably only close to being human. I don't mean to be rude."

"It's all right," she said quickly. She went to the door, opening it. "I understand."

He put a palm on the door to detain her. "I really do appreciate you taking care of everything while I was gone. Though I noticed you didn't take any of the cash I put in the account to pay you."

"I didn't need it. There was really nothing to do. Good night." She hurried out the door, sleet stinging her face. Oh, God, that had been so awkward. It was as if their idyllic time together had never happened.

And yet it had. She was going to have to tell Ty the truth eventually, now that he'd come home. She got in her truck, gazing at the house with rapidly blinking eyes, trying hard to fight back tears.

She missed the Ty who had left BC.

Strangely, irrationally, the Ty who had returned to BC was really hot, dangerous looking. She swallowed, recognizing that her whole body had come alive when he'd walked in the door. So alive she'd forgotten to tell him everything she'd wanted to tell him—even congratulate him on becoming a full-fledged SEAL.

No, in the heat of the moment, caught off guard and worried that her own secrets would somehow be revealed, she'd babbled, saying nothing meaningful.

She hoped he didn't discover that the step had just been repaired. He'd definitely ask questions.

She took a deep, worried breath, astonished that her children were related to Robert Donovan. The thought was shattering. And she'd cut their aunt's hair off, giving Daisy a hairdo that had taken a long time to return to any semblance of attractive.

One thing was crystal clear: Jade wasn't going to make the decision that Honoria had had to make. She would tell him the truth, so that he could know his children.

And hopefully, he wouldn't bring up the marriage promise he'd demanded before he ever even kissed her. She had no desire to be married to a stranger.

And that's what Ty had become.

TY STARED AT the closed door, a little startled by how quickly Jade had disappeared. It was almost unfair how much more beautiful she'd become in his absence. He swallowed, his gut hollowed out by the sudden rush of emotions hitting him since staring into those big green peepers of hers. Peering through the window at her truck, Ty thought about how many cold nights, how many muscle-tearing exercises her smile had gotten him through.

She hadn't smiled at him tonight, not once.

In fact, she'd looked like she'd seen a ghost.

"Hell, maybe I am a ghost," he muttered. He turned to glance through the house once he saw her taillights disappear into the darkness. "A ghost that definitely smells glue."

There was an obvious difference in chemical makeup between glue and dishwashing soap, or even whatever sink cleaner she might have used, and Ty frowned. He left his duffel on the rug and walked into the kitchen, switching on some lights. He'd almost gone to the Hanging H to bunk in with Frog, Squint and Sam, but decided he didn't want anyone to know he was in town just yet. He needed sleep desperately, so desperately he didn't bother to stop at The Wedding Diner to grab a meal, even though he knew there'd be nothing edible in the house, and he missed the hell out of Jane Chatham's home cooking.

He wasn't in the mood for company, needed a few days of sleep to get human again. Once he'd seen Jade's truck parked in his drive, he'd suddenly felt a burst of something he hadn't felt in a long time.

Happiness. He'd been happy as a kid in a candy store to know that little redhead was in his house. She was the only person on this planet he cared to see right now.

"Think I scared her off," he told the salt and pepper shakers on the kitchen island, before turning his gaze to the living room sofa, where he had once held Jade after she'd stumbled down the stairs.

It had been the happiest time of his life, holding that curvy body in his arms.

She'd barely written while he'd been gone, just a few breezy notes reciting the happenings in BC. He'd searched every line she'd penned for the announcement that she was pregnant, and as the months passed, he'd realized her one ovary had been immune to him, after all.

She was even more beautiful now, somehow almost glowing. Something soft and gentle had rounded out her body, and his had responded instantly. If she ever gave him the chance to try to overcome that ovary again, he wouldn't be saying no.

He went to grab a glass of water from the tap, and hesitated, arrested by the dry, clean sink.

Whoa, the little lady had totally tossed off a humdinger of a fib. This sink was clean, but it had not just been cleaned; it was dry as a bone. Even the sponge was dry. He drank the glass of water and walked back to the front door.

Yep. Glue.

His gaze fell to the stair. He'd forgotten all about that, had put the whole thing out of his mind. Bending, he touched the seam, his finger coming away with a trace of wetness. Definitely glue.

She'd waited this long to go through the box and repair the stair? He wiped the glue on his jeans, and thought about why that might be.

They were three weeks from Christmas. Maybe she hadn't had time to do it before—and not sure whether he'd be able to return for the holidays, maybe she'd decided to get on with it.

Which would mean that for nearly a year, she'd just stepped over the broken step.

Shrugging, he decided it didn't matter. She'd done what he wanted done, and he didn't give a damn what was hidden away there. He went back to the kitchen, grabbed a warm beer from a case that was stored in the pantry, cracked it open. Guzzled it, wrinkled his nose, searched out a bottle of whiskey he had in the bar.

"That's more like it," he said, after a satisfying, straight-up gulp. Maybe one more would relax him enough to fall asleep.

He thought about Jade's cloud of soft red hair cascading over her white parka. Maybe she and Sam had gotten together, after all, or maybe someone else had caught her fancy. There was no reason she wouldn't be dating.

Jealousy hit Ty so fast and hard it was stunning. Which was stupid as hell. Why would she wait for him? They'd made no promises to each other, outside of that silly promise he'd extracted from her that if he'd gotten her pregnant, she'd marry him.

Jade would never have married him. She'd been completely focused on his goal.

He'd succeeded in that goal beyond his wildest dreams. Had no regrets.

Except for losing her.

He sat at the kitchen table where he'd eaten meals with his parents. Stared out the window into the back garden, not seeing much thanks to the darkness. Beyond their yard lay Robert Donovan's land, the beginning of his fiefdom. Land that his father had sold Donovan, believing the man when he'd said he wanted to run cattle on it.

Cattle had not been the kingdom Donovan had planned to build. Steel and concrete and a consortium of government-owned buildings was Donovan's plan, turning BC into some kind of outlying big-city-in-the-country—if he could figure out how to push out the hardy, intractable citizens with their thick, stubborn roots buried deep in BC soil.

Ty put the glass to his mouth, hesitating when the doorbell rang and the door swung open.

"Ty?"

He set the glass down at hearing Jade's voice. Sounded like an angel calling to him. Hunger rushed over him, a burning desire he'd never fully extinguished. "In here."

The front door closed, and he waited with his heart hammering. She walked into the kitchen with a huge sack, her red hair windblown and wild, looking like all his dreams come true. Her gaze fell on his nearly empty glass and the whiskey bottle beside it.

"I figured you were hungry."

He was. God, he was hungry. And Little Red Riding Hood had just walked in with her bag of goodies. "I am."

"I stopped at The Wedding Diner and picked you up some food. It won't last you long, but I figured you'd need something." She started unpacking the contents onto the counter. "Pot roast, lasagna or pork roast?"

She glanced at him. His throat dried out.

You. Just you.

"Whichever's easiest. Thanks," he blurted out instead.

"I can't stay," Jade said, pulling out the lasagna. She set it in front of him, retrieved some utensils and put those out, too. "Now, the other two entrées are hot as well, so you're going to have to let them cool before you stick them in the fridge. But you'll have food for the next couple of days if the roads are icy, or you just feel like sleeping." She smiled at him, a smile that electrified him. "I'm putting some of Mom's blackberry cobbler and apple pie in the fridge, too." Jade moved away, a busy whirlwind, intent on her mission. He glanced at the steaming lasagna, but then his gaze ricocheted back to her. That was where his temptation lay, in those round hips, long legs, the sweet smile he remembered so well. "Mom's going to wonder where I am, so I'm off."

He got up, wanting to detain her. But he couldn't. There was a barrier between them that hadn't been there before. So he walked her to the door, following the motion of her sexy butt under the parka with a tight throat. "Appreciate the food."

"Not a problem." She opened the door.

He closed it. "I do have a small question."

She gazed up at him. "Okay."

"I actually have lots of questions." He took a deep breath. "Any chance you'd want to have dinner with me tomorrow night, catch me up on the hometown news?"

The smile slid away, and the shadows he'd seen earlier returned to her eyes. "I can't, Ty."

He nodded. "Okay." His heart plummeted into his stomach.

"Listen," she said suddenly, "eventually we'll talk."

"Eventually?"

"When you've had a chance to sleep. When you've—"

A sudden gust rattled the front windows. Ty opened the door, staring outside. "Snow's really coming down now."

"I have to go." She slipped around him, zipped up her parka on the porch.

"The roads are going to be bad," he warned. "Maybe you should stay here for a while." *Until morning. Sofa, guest room, wherever, just stay.*

"I can't," she said. "Goodbye, Ty."

She went to her truck, got in, switched it on and drove down his drive without looking back.

A lot had changed in eleven months.

He wished it hadn't changed so much.

Chapter Twelve

Jade was still so stunned by Ty's sudden appearance that the next day she kept herself extra busy. The babies, at two months, were starting to become more interested in their surroundings. She set them on the kitchen island counter in their carriers, where they could watch her bake cookies for the Christmas village tonight. Baking would keep her mind off Ty, and it would help out her mother. Jade glanced at her darling girls, cooing at them, still shocked that their grandfather was the horrible, merciless Robert Donovan.

Ugh. The thought made her hands tremble slightly. Jade took a deep breath. "Chocolate-chip cookies it is, girls."

Suz came into the kitchen, her smile huge. "I was hoping these little ladies would be awake! Mwah!" She kissed both babies on their foreheads. "Guess what?" she said to Jade.

"Anything I might guess right now would be wrong," Jade replied. She couldn't have guessed anything that had happened yesterday, from what the box had revealed to Ty suddenly showing up, sending her heart into overdrive.

She was no more over him than she'd ever been.

"We've got the loans on the business paid off!" Suz radiated joy, twirling around the kitchen with an elflike jig. "Robert Donovan can't call them in, can't bulldoze our business, can't hurt us anymore!"

Jade smiled. "That's awesome!"

"It is." Suz finally parked herself on a bar stool so she could play with the babies' toys. "And the guys have promised to stay on another year."

"Frog, Squint and Sam."

Suz nodded, took a few chocolate-chip kisses out of the bag Jade was about to use for the cookies. "This means ol' Mr. Donovan can get *stuffed*."

Jade couldn't help a laugh. "Yes, he can." Probably it was bad of her to speak unkindly of her daughters' grandfather—but then again, he didn't know about them, and what he didn't know didn't hurt him.

Maybe he never had to know.

It's not like he would care, she thought, remembering Sheriff Spurlock's letter to his son.

"Blast," Jade said. "I'm a butterfingers today." She looked at the egg she'd just splattered all over the countertop, the yolk missing the bowl by at least an inch.

Suz grinned. "Guess who's about to come in for a fridge raid?"

Jade stiffened. Surely not Ty.

Oh, she hoped it was Ty. "Who?"

"Who else raids refrigerators like they were personal picnic baskets?" Suz turned to face Sam Barr as he walked in, hands in his jeans pockets, a grin on his handsome face.

Jade was so disappointed it was all she could do to smile.

"Hi, womenfolk," he said cheerfully.

"Womenfolk?" Suz scowled. "Are you a manfolk?"

"I'm not sure. I'll ponder that sometime, princess." He kissed Suz on the cheek, drawing a squeal from her, then dropped a kiss on each baby cheek, as well. Then he looked at Jade, who brandished a wooden spoon at him.

"No, thank you," she said.

He laughed. "You don't know what you're missing."

"I can do without."

"I'd be hurt, except I know you gals who protest the most usually have a secret you're keeping." He went to peer inside the fridge. "Betty said she put some pumpkin pie back just for me. Has my name on it and everything." He foraged around for his treat.

"Well, what about it, Jade?" Suz grinned at her. "Do you have a secret?"

"Not about Sam." Jade shook her head. "I'm sure I have a secret or two, but—"

Sam backed up from the fridge with the pie in his hand, smooching Jade on the cheek before she could pull away.

"You do that again, Sam Barr, and that pie is going in your kisser by a different route than you planned," she promised.

"Phew. Tough case." He sat across the island from her and proceeded to enjoy his pie. "What would you do without me around here?"

"Yes, Jade," Suz said, egging them on. "Did you never figure out that Sam has a huge crush on you?"

Jade looked up from measuring sugar into the bowl, startled. Sam raised a brow, waved a fork dismissively.

"I have a crush on two women in this room, but I'm afraid neither of them is over the age of three months."

He ran a gentle hand over the babies' slightly fuzzy heads. "Sorry, ladies, my heart is taken by these angels."

"Hmm," Suz said, "you're the kind of man who'd set your sights on a woman with a mother who bakes the world's best pumpkin pie." Suz got up to cut a piece of her own.

"I might be that kind of man," he said, winking at Jade, "but I get the pie for free. No need to confuse the process with a wedding ring."

"I'm so disappointed," Jade said wryly. She packed brown sugar into a cup, eyed it carefully. Since neither of them had mentioned Ty's presence in town, she figured he hadn't left the house yet. He was probably sleeping like a fallen log.

"Then again," Sam said, putting his dish in the sink, "that pie is so good I might have to rethink my position." He planted a quick, friendly kiss on Jade's cheek, in the spirit of the teasing.

Suz gasped, then leaped up from the stool, throwing her arms around Ty's neck as he walked into the kitchen, startling Jade so much she nearly dropped the sugar.

"You're back!" Suz exclaimed. "This is going to be a very merry Christmas! Jade, look who it is!"

She was looking—and trying hard not to drink him in as if he were some kind of sexy, exotic cocktail—her eyes caught on Ty's, her heart thundering madly.

Sam went over, slapped him on the back, doing the guy version of greeting. "You old dog! When did you get in?"

Ty grinned at his friend. "Last night."

"Look at you," Suz said. "A real SEAL."

"Hey," Sam said, "*I'm* a real SEAL!"

"You're retired," Suz reminded him. "This one's live and in the flesh."

"Whatever," Sam said, scooping Eve from her carrier. "Look at this, Ty!" He grinned proudly, holding the baby up for Ty's inspection. "Have you ever seen anything so beautiful as these two little ladies?"

Jade froze, wondering how Ty would react. He looked at each baby in turn, his gaze returning to hers. "Congratulations," he said. "They're beautiful."

"That's right," Sam said proudly. "Gonna be rodeo queens one day." He nuzzled Eve's nose. "'Cause I'm planning on rigging the vote if I have to."

Suz laughed. "Cheaters never win."

Ty hadn't broken eye contact with Jade, and she had the feeling something was terribly wrong. She couldn't move—except to pick up Marie, who'd let out a squawk of protest at being left in her carrier.

Then she returned her gaze to Ty's, not sure how to broach the sudden elephant in the room. Suz looked at her strangely, no doubt wondering why she wasn't proudly showing Ty her newborns—only Suz didn't know what Sam had figured out on his own: Ty was a father.

Sam, of course, was no doubt enjoying her discomfort in a friendly, devilish-like-a-brother way.

"Congratulations," Ty said again. "I'm going to head over and see the guys. I just wanted to stop in and thank Betty for all the cookies and candy she sent to me overseas."

He left the kitchen. Suz's jaw dropped. "Wow, what was that all about?"

Jade shook her head, cuddling Marie to her. "Maybe he doesn't like children," she said.

Sam laughed. "Well, he would if they were his."

Jade gave him a warning look. Sam winked again, determined to torture her a little. "The problem is," he said, "Ty left because he thinks these babies are mine."

Suz's gaze flew to Jade. "Are they?"

"No! Oh, for heaven's sake!" She glared at Sam. "Why can't you keep your mouth shut?"

Suz appeared dumbfounded. "Oh, I get it. You mean these babies are…" She stared at Jade. "Ty's the father?" She counted quickly on her fingers. "Oh, my God! Ty is the father!"

Jade shook her head. "I didn't say that." She hadn't wanted anyone to know, hadn't even hinted at it. Betty had backed her on that, saying it was nobody's business.

"Oh, wow," Suz said. "Ty would never have left the country if he'd known you were expecting. And twins!" She gazed at Marie and Eve. "I'm not sure he would have left BC!"

"Exactly." Jade leveled the wooden spoon at Suz and then Sam. "And neither of you is going to tell him."

"You have to tell him," Suz said. "You don't want him thinking that these angels are this knucklehead's." She pointed at Sam. "Ty could be talking about the fact that he was over here, and got to meet Jade and Sam's babies just now. And that would be horrible!"

"Hey!" Sam exclaimed. "I'm a catch! I know I am!"

"You'd be the catch that got tossed back," Suz said.

Jade pulled off her apron, flung it at her friend. "Suz, you mix these cookies for Betty. Just follow the recipe. And Sam, you're on babysitting duty."

"I'd like to complain," he said, "but since I get to graze in Betty's fridge all I like, I'll just sit here with these little pumpernickels and pretend like I'm not the overlooked Prince Charming of BC."

Jade flew out the door, not waiting to hear any more nonsense. It wasn't fair to Ty not to tell him about Eve and Marie. Their old agreement wouldn't be in force any longer—too much had changed. Too much time separated them now.

But he deserved to know the truth—because history shouldn't repeat itself.

Suz STARED AT Sam as he settled himself with another slice of pie and a big cup of frothy organic milk. "I hope you're pleased with yourself."

"Indeed I am." He grinned at her, thinking that for a short stack, she really had a lot of personality. Not his type, of course, but in due time, he could help Frog Francisco Rodriguez Olivier Grant see what he was missing out on. Sam knew when a woman was crushing on a guy, and Suz wore her crush like a beacon, even if she did think she was keeping it on the down-low. "Ah, young love."

Suz narrowed her eyes. "You're going to look like a dunce if you've messed up everything between them. Jade obviously didn't want Ty to know. She didn't want him being tied to BC. She doesn't want him getting himself killed because his mind is on the family he didn't know he had, and the shenanigans back here."

"Tell me about it, cutie pie." Sam munched with contentment, undisturbed by the pot of steam that had become Suz's head.

"You don't have a thing for Jade, do you?" Suz looked at him, mystified, one slim brow raised.

He winked. "I have a thing for you."

"Oh, bull-oney. Bull-*oney*." She shook her head, whacked him on the hand with the wooden spatula, then turned her attention to the recipe she was supposed to be mixing up.

Sam went back to enjoying the pie, his heart completely in love with the luscious blend of creamy pumpkin and cinnamon spreading across his tongue. He had never met the woman who could steal his heart, and knew he never would. Which was why it was so much fun to play matchmaker for his buddies, and watch them fall like babies trying to take their first steps.

"One day, girls," he told Eve and Marie, "one day you're going to get to eat a bite of your granny's pie, instead of sucking on those unsatisfying bottles. And then you'll know why a man will do anything for a woman who cooks like Betty Crocker and Betty Harper. My two favorite ladies."

"Oh, brother," Suz said with disgust. "You have to help me put the holiday decorations up at the Hanging H later. And I don't want any of this nauseating wheezing about how the way to a man's heart is through his stomach."

Sam laughed. "Just don't burn those cookies, cookie, and you and I will get along just fine."

Ty HEADED INTO the bunkhouse at the Hanging H, hoping to find Frog and Squint for some answers. His head whirled, his breath coming too short for comfort. He'd never felt this wound up, not even in Afghanistan.

Jade was a *mother*. And those babies were *tiny*. Two doll-like babies, clearly not that old. He did the math as fast as his poor, stunned brain could manage: They couldn't be more than a few months old, or they'd be bigger.

So those babies weren't his. He'd left in January, so any offspring of his would have been born in October.

Those babies were almost brand-spanking-new.

Damn.

There was no one in the bunkhouse, so he headed over to the main house. He had to have answers. Who was the father?

Of course he knew the answer. Sam had been hanging around, holding a baby, acting very comfortable in Jade's kitchen.

Ty felt as if a huge hole had been blown in his heart. His stomach seemed to be compacted into a cramp he couldn't relax. His dream of coming home to Jade, and the minimal chance that she might have waited for him, faded away.

He opened the back door, as he always had, and five pairs of eyes turned to stare at him, as if he were some kind of specter.

Ty felt like a specter.

Frog, Squint, Mackenzie, Justin and even Daisy hovered around the island, sticking M&M's onto an enormous gingerbread house that covered the entire kitchen island.

"Ty!" Daisy exclaimed. "Welcome home!"

Mackenzie came to hug him, and his buddies slapped him on the back, gave him a punch in the arm and a high five. Daisy gave him a fast hug, then got him a glass of milk and a brownie with peppermint sprinkles on top, pointing him to a bar stool.

"Sit," Mackenzie said, "and tell us everything. We thought you were never coming back to BC!"

God, it was good to be home, among faces that smiled at him and people who loved him. He sat on the bar stool, enjoying the warmth of friends, and briefly wondered why Daisy was in the mix. He hoped like hell Squint hadn't finally decided to fall for her tricks, but Ty had enough problems of his own with a certain fiery redhead.

"Well," Mackenzie prodded, "gobble that brownie, drink that milk and then start with BUD/S. We want to hear about every second from our hometown hero!"

He swallowed hard. He wasn't sure he could push anything past his seriously tight throat. Jealousy seemed to be sitting in his airway like a rock. "Thanks, everybody, for the welcome. It's good to be back."

They grinned, pleased. "We have so much to tell you," Mackenzie said. "But you first!"

"Um, okay." He took a bite, sipped the milk so they wouldn't be disappointed. "Hey, I stopped by the Harper place to check in on Betty and—"

Mackenzie clapped her hands. "And you saw the babies!"

He forced a smile onto his face. "I did, actually."

His friends all looked pleased as could be, as if they were related to the babies or were proud godparents or something. Ty cleared his throat. "Um, Jade didn't mention who the father is, and I didn't really want to pry. What's the story there? She wasn't wearing a wedding ring."

"Well, it's interesting," Frog said. "No one knows who the father is, and we don't have a good guess."

Squint nodded. "We have guesses, but none of them are good."

"Guesses?" Ty swallowed again. "Was Jade dating somebody?"

"No. No one, as far as we know." Squint shrugged. "It's all very mysterious. We have no clue."

"For a while we suspected Sam," Mackenzie said. "But Sam says hell, no. He likes those babies, adores them. Hangs around there all the time."

"Yeah, like a bad smell," Frog said. "But Sam says he hasn't even kissed a girl in BC, and doesn't plan to. Idiot," he added cheerfully. "We were brought here to find brides, weren't we? So why not spread our kisses around?"

They all laughed, relaxed. Ty had a horrible head-ache, all the jovial banter not easing his shock over find-ing Jade had somehow figured out a way to get that ovary working just fine. *Damn, damn, damn.*

"They're so small," he said. "I never saw such deli-cate little things."

Mackenzie grinned. "You should have seen my four when they were born! No bigger than small baking po-tatoes. Want another brownie?"

She put one in front of him, and Ty couldn't say no. It felt so good to be home among his friends—except for the problem with Jade.

"So, buddy," Frog said, "tell us everything."

"When were the babies born?" He had to know.

"October first," Suz said.

His mind went into major mental-math mode. "Oc-tober?" He'd left in January. *My God,* it was possible. Holy hell, it was more than possible that those babies were his. He perked up, feeling a little light suddenly shining into his life—then crashed. Jade had been at his house last night, hadn't breathed a word about babies, a pregnancy, nada. They weren't his. The damning realization crushed his heart. "Jade's never given a hint about who the—"

The back door blew open. Jade came in, stomped the snow off her feet on the mat.

"Hello-o-o, little mama," Frog said. "Join us to welcome home this brave SEAL. And have a fortifying brownie on me!" He gave Jade a big, sloppy smooch on the cheek, which had Ty bristling in spite of himself.

"Hi, everybody. Uh, and Daisy," Jade said awkwardly. "Ty, do you have a second? I need to talk to you."

Everybody looked very interested in her announcement.

"Aha!" Squint exclaimed. "I told you, guys! Ty's the baby daddy!"

They all whooped and carried on something ridiculous around the kitchen island, high-fiving each other and laughing. Ty thought he even might have seen money change hands between Squint and Frog.

"I was sure it was Sam," Frog said. "Until I wasn't sure it was Sam. Then I put my money on a dark horse."

Jade looked embarrassed. Her cheeks got a bit pink and her gaze skittered away from Ty's. "Guys, if you could just go back to building this fine gingerbread house, that'd be awesome."

Well, she hadn't denied that he was the father—that was something. Ty's world spun like mad. Could he be a father? To twins?

That would be the welcome home gift to end all welcome home gifts.

He strode to Jade's side. "Let's go into the fireplace room. If you don't mind, Mackenzie? Justin?"

"Of course not!" They smiled at him demurely—too

demurely. Which tipped him off to the fact that there was a baby monitor on the kitchen island, and it was on.

He reached over and switched it off.

"Aw!" Frog looked chagrined. "We would have turned it off, dude."

"I doubt it. Come on, Jade." Ty led her into the comfortable living room.

"You know they'll turn it right back on."

"Either that or they'll have their ears stuck out to pick up any sound we make. It's like a family of drones." He didn't much care; he was with Jade. It was Christmas, and he couldn't think of any place he'd rather be than here with her, in BC.

"Nice tree," he said to break the tension, tossing a glance over at the beautiful Christmas tree in a corner of the lovely blue-and-white-decorated living room. But that didn't interest him as much as the red-hot mama who took a seat near the fireplace.

"I have to talk to you," she said, and he said, "Yeah, I got that. I'm listening."

His heart thundering, he sat on a sofa, keeping a careful distance between them. He didn't want to get too close, accidentally smell her hair, touch her, have to fight to keep from taking those sweet, cupcake-soft lips.

"First, let me tell you how proud I am that you got your Trident. All of BC celebrated, Ty. It's a huge accomplishment. And everything else you've done, too." She smiled at him and he felt a small glow start inside him—except that she sounded like they were in a job interview and she was about to give him the you're-really-awesome-but-you're-not-quite-right-for-the-job speech.

"Thanks," he said, numbness stealing over him.

"Ty," Jade said, "I became a mother while you were gone."

"I did notice."

"As you know, I wasn't expecting to be able to get pregnant, so it was quite a surprise."

"I'm pretty surprised myself."

He was going to kill Sam. Damn Sam. It had to be him. No one hung around someone's babies, holding them and acting all goo-goo-eyed and mushy, unless they were his own progeny.

Yes, Ty was going to kill Sam, even if he had no rational reason to.

"Congratulations. That's great," he said, realizing something more than what he'd said so far was required. He had to play nice, act pleased for her, cover the fact that he was dying inside.

"I was hoping you'd feel that way."

He nodded, completely destroyed. "I know how much you wanted a baby, Jade. I'm really happy for you."

She took a deep breath. "I just want you to know that our previous agreement obviously isn't necessary. After all, so much has changed. You've been gone nearly a year, and—"

"Agreement?" He was lost, needed a map terribly. Maybe if he wasn't so immersed in her beautiful green eyes he could pay attention better, but he had to hang on to something, and drinking her in was something he'd longed to do for a long time.

"Our marriage agreement." She laughed, sounding somewhat nervous. "We were both in a different place then, and it was a rash agreement."

"Our marriage agreement?"

Her face took on a pink cast, and he realized she was embarrassed.

"I shouldn't have brought it up. Never mind. Forget I said anything."

"Hang on a minute." He held up a hand. "What are you talking about, Jade?"

She looked at him, obviously torn about saying more.

"Don't leave me in the dark." He glanced at the Christmas tree twinkling in its corner and scratched his head. "I remember saying that if you happened to get pregnant, I wanted to marry you."

"Yes." She looked relieved. "But you don't have to anymore."

Finally they were getting someplace. "Won't the father marry you? I mean, if Sam's being an asshole, I can sure beat his head in for you."

Her eyes went wide. "Sam's not the father of my children. Sam doesn't want any part of marrying anyone, and he certainly wouldn't get a woman pregnant. He avoids what he calls women traps like the plague. For that matter, so do Squint and Frog—even if they claim to be here looking for brides. I just don't think they're all that serious. Playing the field, is my guess."

"Back to the father issue." Ty couldn't get the whole story straight in his head. "We'll worry about the home team and their field-playing later."

"The babies are yours, Ty," Jade said softly, and it felt as if wings rushed into his heart, lifting it skyward.

"Mine?"

She frowned. "Well, of course! Who else's would they be?"

He swallowed hard, stunned. "I don't see how."

She raised a brow. "You don't see how?"

"We don't, either," Frog called down the hall. "Can we have a few more details? There's a big hole in this story!"

Jade grabbed Ty's hand, led him down the hall to a guest room, closed the bedroom door. "Of course you're the father. You don't remember working really hard to help me get pregnant?"

She looked seriously disappointed in him, so Ty reached out, pulled her to him. "Slow down a minute, beautiful, and let me catch my breath. I'm still processing the fact that I don't have to tie Sam to a cactus and leave him for an unpleasant, prickly end."

"I can't believe you think Sam and I... I mean, I would never—" Jade looked at him, disgusted. "No. Never Sam. He's just really good with the babies, and he loves them. And I think they're comforted by his deep voice. Actually, the girls love Frog and Squint, too, but they don't come around daily, even hourly, like Sam does."

Ty grunted. "I'll try to thank him. Won't be easy, because I'm a bit jealous." If those tiny little pink-wrapped babies were his, he was totally jealous of all the hours Sam had spent holding them that he had missed out on. "So, mine, huh?"

"Of course they are. I just didn't tell you because I was...afraid."

Ty gazed into her eyes, seeing her apology in her honesty. "Because of my training."

"I really felt like it was best if I waited until later to tell you. I'm sorry if I did the wrong thing." Jade took a deep breath. "Believe me, it wasn't the easiest decision I ever made."

He pulled her into his arms. "I'm a father. That's just

about the best welcome-home gift I could have ever gotten. I don't know if it's totally hit me yet."

She smiled. "Sometimes the fact that I'm the mother of twins hasn't totally hit me yet, either."

"Twins." His brain struggled to take that information in. Then he laughed out loud. "I told you your ovary would like me."

She tried not to laugh, moved out of his arms. "Yes, you did. Crow all you like. You deserve it."

"I certainly plan to. So now, about getting married—"

"No, no. That's exactly what I came here to tell you." Jade's face turned serious. "Marriage is out of the question."

Chapter Thirteen

Ty hurried after Jade as she exited the bedroom. "What do you mean, out of the question? Of course we're getting married! Those babies are going to have a father, and it's not going to be Stand-in Sam!"

Jade stopped in the hallway and put a hand against Ty's chest, sending his pulse skyrocketing. He wanted to kiss her desperately, celebrate his good fortune of becoming a father—sensed that would be a mistake. Jade was far too defensive, her demeanor closed off from him.

Nope. No kissing.

But as soon as he could manage it, he was going for those sweet lips. He'd gone far too long without kissing Jade.

"I don't want anything to change, Ty."

He caught her hand in his. "Sorry, darling, it's changing."

"It can't." Jade shook her head, adamant. "Ty, look. I spent the last several months eaten up with guilt because I wasn't telling you that you were a father. I didn't know if that was the right decision or not. What if you'd died? Gotten killed by a roadside bomb or something?" Her eyes filled with tears, astonishing him. "You have no idea how hard it is to watch the news every night with your heart in your throat, wondering if your babies are ever going to get to know their father."

Their friends trooped out of the kitchen.

"Ty's really the father?" Squint asked. "I did not see that coming."

"I thought about it once," Frog said, "but I dismissed it as being too impossible."

"Oh, wow," Mackenzie said. "What a great home-coming gift for you, Ty!"

"Congratulations, Ty," Daisy said, and he wondered again why his friends had suddenly let trouble into their tight-knit circle.

"That's awesome!" Mackenzie flew down the hall to throw her arms around his neck. "Now Justin will have a fellow father to talk baby with!" She glanced with delight at her husband, and he saluted Ty with a grin.

"Uh, yeah. I hadn't exactly thought of it that way, but yeah. Me and Justin. Fathers. Who would have ever thought it?" Ty said, feeling a little panic come over him. But he wasn't going to be a husband, not like Justin. The sparky redhead who'd drifted into the kitchen with the rest of the group seemed pretty clear on that.

"Excuse me, gang," he said, following Jade as she tried to sneak out the back door. "Just a minute, mother of my children."

Jade kept walking toward her house. "I have to get back. It's almost time to nurse the babies."

"I can help you." He was damned if Sam would be Drop-In Daddy any longer, not while he was around.

"Not with nursing, you can't." Jade walked faster. "Ty, I get that all of this is a shock to you, and you're welcome to come around anytime you like to see the babies, but I don't want anything to change between us. I mean it."

He caught her hand, stopping her. "As I said, everything has changed. So get ready for that." It felt so good to hold her hand, hold any part of her, that he forgot his earlier vow about keeping his distance, and pulled her against his chest. "Now *this* feels like home."

She remained against his chest, surprising him, because he'd expected a bit of a tussle. She was plenty strong-willed, and he'd been gone long enough to give her time to get really set in her ways. "I know you have some bug in your head about me, and the babies, but we're getting married, beautiful."

She pulled away. "I can't marry you. I'm sorry."

"Because?" He stopped her when she prepared to dart off again. "Because you don't want to be married to a guy who's not going to be around much?"

"Of course not!" She thumped his chest with a stern finger. "No one has supported your dreams more than me, so don't even go there."

"Then why? Marrying me is the smartest thing you could do. We have babies who need the Spurlock name."

She seemed to go a little pale, though it was hard to tell in the very frigid weather, which was already pinkening her cheeks. "Oh, God, Ty."

"What?" He looked at her. "What is it?"

"I can't marry you. I'm sorry, I can't. I appreciate that you want to do the right thing by the children, but I promise you, Eve and Marie will be just fine."

He stopped, his brain scrambling. "Eve and Marie?"

"Yes." She looked at him curiously. "Didn't I tell you?"

"I might have missed it, but—" He tried on his daughters' names, turning them over in his mind. "Those are beautiful names. Eve and Marie Spurlock. Perfect."

"No," Jade said, "they're Eve and Marie Harper. It's just the way it has to be."

She headed off, her boots crunching in the crusty snow.

"Why?" He stopped her again. "A promise is a promise, doll face, and you did promise me that marriage was my reward for overcoming your timid ovary."

She shook her head. "Neither of us knew what we were promising then, Ty. Forget it."

"I'm not forgetting a damn thing. My daughters are going to have my name."

Jade sighed. "Ty, how much more bad news do you want in one day?"

"Bad news?" He considered that. "I haven't had any bad news today. All I've gotten is good news, so go ahead and hit with me with whatever you're keeping under that sexy red hair of yours. Be prepared, you're talking to a navy SEAL. I don't hear a whole lot of bad news. Everything filters into best possible outcomes."

"All right." Jade took a deep breath. "I didn't want to tell you this. I know you said you didn't want to hear, and God knows, I'm still pretty floored by the whole thing. But I finally opened that stupid box."

"So? Nothing that was buried in a box is going to keep me from being a father to my children, Jade." He tucked her against his chest once more, wanting to chase away the sudden shadows in her eyes. "I promise you, everything is going to be fine. I suggest you start thinking of what kind of wedding gown you'll be wearing."

"Ty, I don't really know how to say this," she said,

pulling herself from his arms, "but Robert Donovan is the girls' grandfather."

Ty stared at her, caught and wary. "No, he's not. Not if I'm the father."

"You're the father," Jade said slowly, softly. It came to him that she was trying very gently to point him toward information she thought he needed. "And Robert Donovan is your father."

The earth shifted beneath his feet, then Ty realized it was his legs going rubbery. His brain felt rubbery, too, unable to process what the mother of his children had just said. "What?"

She took another deep breath. "Ty, I'm so very sorry. Sheriff Spurlock and your mother adopted you from Robert Donovan's wife. Robert doesn't even know you're his son. That's why the box was buried. Your father never intended anyone to know." Jade's eyes filled with sympathetic tears. "I so didn't want to tell you, Ty. I know you said you never wanted to know what was in it, and I tried to keep to the letter of our agreement. But as you can see, that's a promise I just can't keep."

He shook his head, refusing to acknowledge what he was hearing. Felt himself grow dark inside. It explained so much. God, how he despised Donovan. Almost hated him.

This was insanely bad news. "So Daisy is my sister."

Jade nodded. "I invited her to come to a few more of our functions and projects, Ty. It's not easy for me. But there's a part of me that feels that family should be...family."

"I don't see how. She's as evil as her father." He straightened. "So I'm evil, too."

"Not hardly. Of course you're not!" She rushed into

his arms to comfort him. "Don't say that! You're one of the most admired men in this town."

He shook his head. "Jade, you don't understand. I'm more Donovan than I am Spurlock."

"You're pure Spurlock. Nurture versus nature. You know that."

"I don't know that." He had a dark side, he knew. Now he understood where that darkness came from.

"Look, that's a silly theory. If I gave my babies to Cosette Lafleur to raise, they'd grow up very artsy, thinking pink hair was normal, and chatting in French. Of course you're your father's son! Sheriff Spurlock was a fine man, and so are you."

Ty's whole world had changed, sliding into some kind of strange abyss he hated. He couldn't take it in. "You're positive that's what was in the box?"

"I'm afraid so." Jade backed away, feeling horrible for him, not sure how to comfort him. "I really didn't want to tell you, but I'd already kept one thing from you, which I felt horribly guilty about, and still do. I couldn't keep two secrets that would change your life."

"I know." He shook his head. "I'm not angry with you. I'm just cursed."

"You're not cursed! That's ridiculous!"

"I'm going," Ty said suddenly, making up his mind. "I'm going to see the babies."

She looked worried. "And then what?"

He walked away, no longer sure.

But one thing he did know—he was going to be a father that his daughters knew loved them.

TY COULDN'T SAY he was relieved to know that the reason Jade didn't want to marry him had to do with his newfound family lineage, and her own feelings of remorse over keeping things from him. Part of those guilty feelings he could have honestly told her to forget about—he'd insisted he didn't want to know what his father had hidden away in the staircase, and he wasn't sorry about that decision at all.

In fact, a big part of him wished he still didn't know. He was surprised by the amount of anger that had rushed into him at her revelation—anger and questions and fury. But not with her. All his fury was directed at Robert Donovan, who apparently had been an ass for so many years that even his own wife hadn't trusted him.

The anger Ty would deal with later.

As for Jade, just worrying about why she'd been keeping him at arm's length had been plenty to have on his mind. But now that he knew, he agreed with her; there could be no marriage between them. The last thing he was going to do was sully his daughters' lives and reputations by announcing their relationship to Robert Donovan.

God, what a hellish curse that would be to live under.

And it wasn't a secret that could be kept. Right now, their dearest friends knew that Ty was the father of Jade's babies. Daisy had been in the room with the others, so by now, all of BC had heard the news. That was how secrets worked in their community—they just didn't stay buried forever.

It sucked, really sucked, to know that Donovan was his birth father. And yet Ty could be a better man than Donovan; the curse didn't have to perpetuate itself.

"Listen," he said suddenly, as Jade returned to the kitchen, where he'd sat himself at the table. He'd tried to nibble on one of Betty's oatmeal-raisin cookies, but frankly, his appetite was gone like the wind. "Has Sam left?"

She nodded, sat across from him. "One look at your face seemed to convince him that his presence wasn't needed. He shot out of here and didn't even give me a report on the babies." Jade smiled at Ty and selected a cookie for herself. "Sam usually likes to give me the rundown of every single thing the girls have done while he was babysitting, from first poop to possible smile."

"Yeah, well." Jealousy sparked inside Ty again. "While I'm here, I don't want Sam babysitting. I'll babysit." He pondered that for a second. "I guess it's not babysitting if I'm the father. Then it's probably dad-sitting or something."

"Fine by me."

"So anyway." He took a deep breath. "You and I are going to keep this deep, dark secret, okay? For as long as we can, anyway. I don't want the girls growing up with a shadow hanging over their heads. You have to admit it's a big, nasty shadow. I don't know how long something like this can stay hidden. Part of me wonders if there's another shoe that might drop." Or someone else who knew.

"I leave that decision up to you, although part of me wonders if Robert has the right to know."

"He has the right to nothing." Ty got up, paced the room. "He'd figure out a way to use them to get something he wants. Trust me, I know the man. He's an open book. When it comes to his ambition, everyone is a sacrifice."

"Except Daisy."

"I'm not so sure." Ty sat down at the table again, reached for Jade's hand, held it between his. "For now, let's agree that particular skeleton stays buried in the closet."

"Staircase," she murmured. "Fine by me. I sealed that box up tight. Very tight."

"Why'd you wait so long to look in the box?"

Jade shrugged. "It was your personal business."

Ty stared at her. "You realize you may be the only woman on the planet who doesn't have killer curiosity. I'm betting any other one would have looked that first night."

"I waited in case you didn't make it through BUD/S. If you'd decided to come home, then I could have made you do it—"

"Ha! You were the one who told me to stay in training no matter what!" Ty squeezed her fingers lightly.

"I know. But being a SEAL isn't for everyone."

"You think I can't do what Squint, Sam and Frog did? I don't know that I appreciate your lack of faith," he teased.

"I just thought I'd wait to see what happened." Jade pulled her fingers from his, got up to get coffee. "And then I was pregnant. The last thing on my mind was the box, and I kind of forgot about it. I went over to your house once a week, but I'd put the stair back together, and taped it off so Betty would know which one to avoid."

"Your mother's been going to my house, too? And you didn't tell her about the box?"

"Nope." Jade poured them each a cup, set one in front of him. "I told her you had mentioned the stair came loose, and that we were supposed to be careful. I don't think Mom paid any attention. When I was put on bed rest in the sixth month, she went over there all the time in my place."

"I'll thank her later," he said gruffly. "I didn't mean to cause trouble for your whole family. I was trying to take care of you in case something happened to me." He scowled. "You didn't touch a dime of the money in the account, but you had my daughters! You should have taken some of the money to help raise my children. Why else does a man bother to draw up a will except to take care of his responsibilities?"

Ty wasn't satisfied with her clear-eyed gaze, which stubbornly reminded him that she could take care of herself. "Anyway, you should have written to tell me," he grumbled, knowing very well why she hadn't. "Were you going to tell me when they were walking down the aisle with their husbands?"

"I was going to tell you when I knew it was safe to do so," Jade said. "Now drink your tea and get warmed up before I kick you out. It's almost time for me to nurse. The girls will be awake any second."

"I want to meet them. I barely glanced at them earlier. I think I was in shock." He shook his head, remembering the punch in his gut at seeing the babies. "I know I was in shock."

"You'll meet them. Soon."

"I will today," he said stubbornly, walking around the table to take the seat next to her. He held her close against him, putting his face against her neck, sighing with happiness. "I thought constantly about the way you smell. I dreamed of your red, springy hair and your sweet lips that kiss me like I'm the only guy in the world."

She tried to wriggle away, but he was having none

of it. "You just sit still, beautiful. I came a long way to hold you, and I plan to do it often. Now that the whole town knows you've had my children, I figure there's no need to hide my feelings for you."

Jade turned to gaze into his eyes. "You're not angry?"

He kissed her neck, taking his time. "Oh, I'm a little peeved. I underestimated your desire and ability to keep secrets. I wish you'd told me about the babies. It would have given me something to occupy my mind with."

"I didn't want you occupying your mind with anything but staying alive." Jade got up, moved to the counter to refill her cup, but he knew she was just creating distance. A little squeak came over the monitor, and a serenely happy look settled over Jade's face, hitting Ty like an arrow shot into his heart.

He'd never seen anyone appear so joyful, so peaceful. She was thrilled to be a mother.

"You get to meet your daughters now, although I'm going to warn you, it's not a romantic thing. It's dirty diapers and spit-up—"

"Lots of things in the navy make me think I can handle a little baby hurl. Lead on," he said drily.

She went down the hall and he followed her into a nursery where a night-light glowed softly and the scent of baby powder hung in the air. He could see two small heads barely moving, and a tiny hand flailing.

"Girls, this is your daddy," Jade said, picking a baby up from the crib where *Eve* was scrolled in delicate letters. "Eve, meet SEAL Ty Spurlock, your father and one of the finest men I've ever known."

He took the baby, memorizing everything in that first touch. Eve was warm from sleeping, her tiny body a little taut from the wail she wanted to let fly, until he held her to his chest. Then she went still, surprised by the new arms cuddling her.

"And this is Marie." Jade held the other baby and unbuttoned her blouse as she sat in a rocker. "If you walk around with Eve, she'll stay calm until I've got Marie fed."

"Second fiddle, are you?" he murmured to the baby, and Jade laughed.

"No, she just has my patience. Marie has your impatience."

"I don't think I'm impatient." Of course he was. Nothing ever moved fast enough or smoothly enough to suit him. "Okay, I'm impatient."

Jade smiled. "I'm glad you came home."

He cleared his throat, still kind of lost in the soft, sweet scent of his daughter and the warmth of her tiny body against his chest. He was lost in the beauty of Jade nursing his other daughter, and the love sweeping over him as he realized that this was the most amazing moment of his life.

He was a father. A real father. He had two daughters, and the three females in this room had just become his entire world.

"We're going about this all wrong. You're going to have to marry me," Ty said, his tone tight with emotion. "I know you've got a thousand bugs in your brain because of the way that everything happened, and the secrets that you had to keep for so long, but babe, if you don't marry me, these little girls are going to grow up thinking their father is a lightweight in the dad department." He kissed Eve, loving the tiny, downy hairs that sparsely adorned her head. Then he stared his stubborn lady down. "I did my part, angel face. Now it's time for you to do yours."

Chapter Fourteen

The wedding was a fast, beautiful affair that took place right before Christmas. Jade couldn't believe how quickly everything was happening. After lots of soul searching, she and Ty had agreed that marriage was the right thing for the children.

They'd never talked about love. But she did love Ty, with all her heart and soul. She understood why he hadn't mentioned it, though it pained her a little. Until Ty came to terms with who he was—the new him he'd just discovered—she didn't figure he could love anyone.

Except the babies. Oh, how he loved Eve and Marie. Jade smiled as she took off the cream-colored gown she'd worn to the courthouse. Ty had insisted the girls be at the wedding. He'd held Eve and she'd held Marie, and thankfully, the ceremony had been swift, because Jade had been nervous the girls would get cranky and her breasts would start leaking.

Funny thing to worry about on one's wedding day. But she had bigger things on her mind now, the biggest of which was the fact that she knew good and well that Ty hadn't completely forgiven her for not telling him he was a father.

He hadn't said much about it, but she sensed it was

in the back of his mind. Trust was a huge factor in a relationship, and when he'd just learned he was related to people with whom the word *trust* was never associated, he needed to be able to count on someone, absolutely.

She'd have to build that up in their marriage.

"Hurry up!" Betty called from the bottom of the stairs. "It's time to cut the cake. The natives are restless!"

Jade sent one last appraising glance over the red velvet dress she'd bought months ago at the maternity store, glad it covered the full curves she was working on diminishing just a bit, and hurried down the stairs.

"My goodness, is all of BC here?" she asked Ty, who looked quite pleased with himself as he held his daughters in his arms.

"Wedding cake at Christmastime. Nobody in town is ever going to pass that up."

"As the best man, I'll pass the cake," Frog said. "That way I make sure I get the biggest piece."

Everyone booed him playfully, and Betty gave her a slight nudge toward the cake. Jade picked up the knife and glanced at her husband. "I think the way this works is that I'm supposed to cram some of this into your mouth."

He grinned. "Do your worst, Mrs. Spurlock."

She jumped at hearing her new name on his lips, and everyone gathered in the dining room crowed with delight.

"I'll pass the plates around," Suz said, coming forward. "Here, you take a baby," she told Mackenzie, handing her Eve. "And you take the other munchkin, Daisy. It might just stir something warm in your heart."

Jade froze, and beside her, she felt Ty do the same.

They watched as Daisy took little Marie, cooing to her. It was astonishing to watch Daisy act as if she actually didn't mind holding an infant, even was happy to be included. Jade looked at Ty uncomfortably, and after a moment, he shrugged.

There was no point in being ugly in front of everyone in BC. People were standing six deep in the dining room and were spilled out on the lawn. Jade put a smile on her face. "I'm going to cut as fast as I can, and you guys make an assembly line of sorts. Grab your cake and then head into the den area, where the Christmas tree is, so everyone can make it in out of the cold."

That seemed to be a plan the crowd liked—as long as they got cake—and Jade cut the first slice. "Here goes," she told Ty, and carefully put a piece into her husband's mouth.

"Excellent cake, Betty and Jane," he said, "but I know one thing that's sweeter." He gave Jade a big smooch on the lips that had everyone laughing.

"Help me with this," she said, wiping a little frosting from his face.

She and Ty sliced the cake swiftly, and Mackenzie and Betty passed it along to grateful wedding guests, all of whom had congratulatory words to say to their hometown son and daughter. Jade couldn't stop smiling. Why had she worried? This was turning out to be one of the most magical days of her life. It was so hard to believe that this big, strong, handsome man was now her husband. How many years had she dreamed of this very moment?

"You got off easy, you know, old son," Squint said as he passed by. "The folks are grousing that you got set up with a bride and didn't even have to swim the creek."

Ty grinned. "That's right. No Bridesmaids Creek swim for me to find a bride. I got mine without magic."

"Yeah," Sam said, "you didn't have to navigate Best Man's Fork, either. The folks feel a bit cheated."

"That's just fine." Ty laughed, and Jade loved the sound of it. Just hearing him so relaxed and happy gave her hope for their marriage, as strange as it had started out. "I've run the fork and swum that creek so many times training for BUD/S that the magic already did its thing." He gave Jade another smooch, and people laughed. She had just turned to finish cutting the last several slices of the lovely three-tiered confection trimmed with gold roses and latticework when the room went totally silent.

So silent it felt as if everyone quit breathing.

Robert Donovan walked in, a plate of cake in his hand, a big grin on his face. Jade froze. Beside her, she felt Ty go totally tense, protective in his stance near her.

"Donovan," Ty said. "You didn't have an invite."

"Don't need one." He glanced at the guests, his gaze falling on each person's face, which somehow felt threatening. Jade was glad the babies had been taken into the den by Cosette and Phillipe.

Daisy came into the room. "Dad, what are you doing here? Weddings aren't your thing."

"Everyone likes a wedding." He grinned hugely, sort of nastily, and Jade wondered if that was just Robert Donovan's normal expression. Looking at him, knowing his history, made her sick to her stomach.

"That's it," Betty said, bustling into the kitchen. "Out you go, Donovan. This is my house, and you aren't invited. And there are still laws we follow in this town about trespassers."

"That's interesting, Betty. You're just the person I came here to see." He glanced around. "Now that your only chick's going to move out, you won't need a place this big. Ten acres is far too much for you to handle."

"Don't see that's any of your business," Jade's mother snapped.

"It's connected to the Hanging H. Only divided by a fence," Robert said. "Makes it very valuable, Betty. I could make you a nice offer. In fact, I'm making you a very nice offer. A property like this could easily go for a million dollars."

The guests who had filed back into the dining room to see what was going on gasped. Betty put her hands on her hips, frowning. "Donovan, if that's all you came to say on the day of my daughter's wedding, then get the hell out."

He looked at her like a cat about to pounce on a bird. "Betty, you don't want to be out here all by yourself."

"*Your* chick hasn't flown the coop," Betty snapped. "Anyway, even when mine does, I'll be just fine."

"A lot can happen to an elderly woman in a place this big," Robert said, and everyone gasped again.

"That's enough," Ty said. "You've had your say. Betty's asked you to leave, so I suggest you do so before we help you."

Sam, Squint, Justin and Frog came to stand at Ty's side for backup, a scrum of dangerous-looking men. Jade breathed an internal sigh of relief.

Robert glanced around the room. "A fall, a broken hip. You'd be much better off in a smaller place, Betty. Now where are those tiny newcomers to Bridesmaids Creek I've heard so much about? No bigger than Christmas stockings, apparently, since they were born a few weeks early. Not too healthy, are they? A million dollars could make a lot of difference in their lives."

Jade caught Ty's arm to keep him from jumping across the table and punching Donovan. Her husband was not going to jail on their wedding day.

"Robert Donovan, let me ask you something," Betty said, getting right up close to him so she could poke his chest with her finger. "What's all the empire building about, anyway? You can't take any of this with you when you go."

"I don't have to. I have my daughter." He glanced at Daisy, but strangely, she didn't smile back at him. In fact, Jade thought she looked mortified by her father's behavior. "She'll inherit everything."

"Really," Betty said. "Well, maybe she won't. Maybe all your empire building is for nothing."

The whole room went silent.

"What do you mean, Betty Harper?" Donovan growled.

"I just mean that you might find your empire being split up one day." She poked him again. "So if was you, I'd mind myself."

"I don't have any other heirs," Donovan said.

"I'm tired of you, Robert," Betty said. "I'm tired of you scaring folks half to death in this town because they're afraid you're going to buy up the debt on their ranches and their homes, and call the loans on them. I'm tired of you running roughshod over everyone, and hurting people, and ruining every damn thing this town's tried to build. So here's a little news flash for you. You do have other heirs, and they happen to be my granddaughters. How does it feel to know that kingdom you're building isn't exactly the one you thought it was?"

Jade stiffened. "Mother!"

"He deserved it," Betty said. "I'm sorry, I—"

Ty leaped on Robert Donovan, throwing a right hard enough to knock the older man down. The entire room had gone deathly silent as Daisy stared at Jade and asked the question everyone wanted answered.

"Is it true?" Daisy demanded.

THE GUESTS HAD left in a hurry after Donovan was helped to his feet. He'd been carted off to the hospital, and Jade didn't care even if he did need to have his jaw reattached to his face. He deserved it for the many miseries he'd caused everyone in BC for so many years.

But her mother—oh, God, what was she going to do about her mother? Ty hadn't spoken a word to Jade since Betty's big reveal—in fact, he'd been the one to take Donovan to the hospital.

Ty had barely looked at Jade or Betty when he'd left, with Squint, Frog and Justin following him for backup. Probably to keep him from murdering Donovan on the way to the hospital.

"Mom!" Jade exclaimed when Betty bustled into the room. "Mom, what were you thinking?"

"I wasn't." Betty took off her apron. "The girls are asleep in the nursery, completely worn out from their big day." She looked at her daughter as Suz and Mackenzie came into the room to help carry dishes to the kitchen. "Well, yes, I was thinking. I was thinking just how badly I'd like to see Donovan get his just deserts."

"You had no right, Mom!" Ty was never going to speak to Jade again; she just knew it. He'd been adamant that the girls' true parentage remain a secret forever.

But even he had noted that secrets didn't stay buried in BC.

"How did you even find out about that, anyway?" Jade demanded.

"I heard you two talking over the baby monitor," Betty said, looking shamefaced. "You didn't know I'd come in the front door. I went down to check on the girls in the nursery, and I heard. I switched the monitor off as soon as I could, but it was too late. I am sorry for eavesdropping." Her shoulders drooped. "In fact, I'm sorry for spoiling your big day." She shook her head, collapsing onto a sofa with a sigh. "I guess I'm not as good as folks always try to paint me to be. But Lord, he got my nerves up, and I just wanted to pop that fat head off his fat neck!"

Jade sighed, sank onto the sofa next to her mother. "It was a beautiful cake and a lovely wedding day. I know you worked hard to pull all this together for me."

Betty put her head on her daughter's shoulder. "You know, I think it was all Robert's horrible talk about me getting old, and falling, and being helpless, and my daughter leaving my roost. And my grandbabies." She wiped at her eyes. "I think the old goat hit me on so many of my worst fears that I just wanted to give him a taste of his own medicine. Let him know he wasn't the big dog he thinks he is, and that this is one town he can't rule like some kind of king. We've got spirit here that he can't crush!" She gave a dramatic sigh. "I am so sorry, Jade. This town will be talking about your wedding day until the end of time."

"Yes, it will." Jade couldn't help smiling at her mother's statement, despite her forlorn tone. "Let's not worry about it anymore. What's done is done."

"Yes, but my son-in-law is going to think I'm a dragon. He tore out of here like a tornado was after him."

"Daisy went with him. They can have some bonding time."

"I doubt it very seriously. That's a brother-sister duo that isn't going to gel very quickly." Betty sat up. "Anyway, we have the girls. As far as I can see, you're sitting in the catbird seat, Jade Harper Spurlock."

"What do you mean?"

"It means," Betty said, "that Robert Donovan can't touch you. Can't threaten you, can't make your life miserable. You've got his granddaughters, and it could be years before Daisy gives him any bundles of joy!"

"Mom, Ty doesn't want our daughters anywhere near Donovan. I doubt very seriously Mr. Donovan would want any part of them, either. They're not going to be part of the Bridesmaids Creek power struggle."

"Doesn't matter. Everything changes for that smug old goat now." Betty giggled, sounding a whole lot less remorseful.

"Yes, and everything changes for me, too," Jade reminded her. "My husband's reeling from everything that's happened since he got home. This was supposed to be a simple holiday leave. Now he'll go back a different man than he was before he came home."

"Yes. But you're different, too." Betty shrugged. "When you read that letter, your life changed, too, Jade."

"Mom, you eavesdrop far too well." She sighed. It didn't matter now. All the cats were out of their flimsy bags. In her heart, she'd known that Ty was right: secrets didn't stay buried forever, not these kinds of secrets, anyway.

"You realize that your marriage stole a little bit of

Madame Matchmaker's thunder." Betty got herself a piece of cake, plopped down next to her daughter, taking a bite with a sigh of pleasure. "Not bad cake, if I do say so myself."

"I think Cosette understands that things just happened."

"She likes to wave her magic wand, though. I feel like the Lafleurs might get back on a solid marital footing if they had some good luck, and that matchmaking business of theirs is key. I've been thinking this over, and I know how we can make things better for her and Phillipe." Betty grinned. "We're going to let her work her matchmaking magic on *Daisy*."

Jade got herself a piece of cake, too, figuring she might as well enjoy another slice, since she was the bride. "But Daisy and who? I don't even have a good idea for that."

"We'll let Cosette handle that little snare."

"To what end?" Jade wondered. "Daisy doesn't want to get married, and I haven't heard anyone but Squint mention he'd want to tangle with that whirlwind."

Betty straightened. "Not Squint. He's too nice. Too damaged. He needs something good in his life—not Daisy Donovan and her gang of wild men."

"And then there're those guys." Jade licked her fork. "Whoever marries her is going to have to put up with her gang. They're not exactly a barrel of monkeys, and I'm pretty sure every one of them is on Robert's payroll over and beyond the work that they do for his kingdom, as you referred to it."

"I thought that was inspired." Betty beamed. "Maybe I'll go into the wedding-cake business."

"Mom, you don't have any time to do one more thing."

"You know what I wish? I wish you'd had time for a honeymoon." Betty shook her head. "You know, your father and I went to Oklahoma for ours. We camped out under the stars. It was nice."

Jade wasn't sure Ty had even thought about a honeymoon. There wasn't time before he went back to his military service, and besides, she was still nursing.

She just wanted her marriage to be a real one, and the look on Ty's face today when Betty had spilled the beans—okay, flung the whole pot of beans right at Robert's head—hadn't boded well. "I'm glad Dad and you had a lovely honeymoon. And I'm sure Ty and I will do something, one day."

Betty set her plate on the coffee table. "I'm going to start cleaning up. I want you to do nothing but be a bride today. Suz and Mackenzie can help. You just relax."

"I'm not going to relax," Jade said, getting up with her. "All the fun's in the kitchen."

Betty hugged her. "Be mad at me, but don't be mad at me forever. I couldn't bear it. Robert was right, I dread the thought of my darling chick leaving me. You might move to another state to be with that hunky SEAL husband of yours. I would if I was you."

"I don't think so." She relaxed into her mother's hug, enjoying the love. "I'm not sure what Ty's got in mind. And I'm not mad at you. I'm astounded by what you did, but then again, you're my mother. I suppose the apple didn't fall far from the tree."

The back door flew open and Daisy marched in, her long, chocolate hair flying.

"I hope you're both happy!" She glared at them.

"Sit down, Daisy," Jade said, recognizing that her new sister-in-law was in a twirl. "Let me get you a nice, hot cup of tea. It's really cold outside."

Daisy didn't sit, didn't move. The glare in her eyes could have frozen water. "I hope you're both happy with the way you behaved today. Very happy."

"Look, Daisy, it wasn't—" Jade began, but Betty put a hand on her arm.

"What's wrong, Daisy?" Betty asked.

Daisy's dark eyes blazed. "My father's had a heart attack, and it's all your fault! You just couldn't keep your big mouth shut. You had to tell all those horrible lies!" She looked completely wild and unsettled. "You've always been horrible and mean, Jade, you and Mackenzie and Suz. You're regular queen bees." Daisy burst into tears, something Jade had never seen her do.

"Now, girlie," Betty said, but Daisy rounded on her.

"Don't you say a word! This is all your fault! You just had to be horrible, and if my father dies, I'm going to, well, I don't know what!"

"You're upset, Daisy, and rightfully so. Sit down here and rest a minute." Jade steered her to a chair at the table. "Tell us what happened."

She quickly got a plate of wedding cake and some cookies, putting them in front of Daisy. Betty grabbed the teakettle and poured a cup of hot water for tea, setting a floral cup next to the sweets.

"You know what happened. Your horrible husband practically shattered my dad's jaw—"

"Shattered?" Jade asked.

"Well, no," Daisy said. "It's just badly bruised, the doctor says."

Jade let out a breath, glancing at her mother before she sat down across from Daisy. "And the heart attack?"

"Well, it's not actually a heart attack. It's a severe attack of angina. Brought on by stress!" She glared at Betty, then scarfed a cookie in record time. Started in on the wedding cake. "Mmm, this is good. Maybe I'll hire you to make my cake when I get married."

Jade raised a brow. "Are you getting married?"

"Do you think I'm going to let your daughters become my father's sole heirs after me?" Daisy asked.

"I don't expect that your father cares anything at all about my children," Jade shot back.

"He will. Dad's all about progeny and the future-generations thing." Daisy sighed. "I'm thinking about Francisco. Wouldn't Mr. and Mrs. Francisco Rodriguez Olivier Grant look nice on wedding invitations?"

Jade and Betty both gawked. "Frog?" Jade asked. "Why him?"

"He's ripe for the picking." Daisy shook her head. "Then again, Squint isn't hard on the eyes. It's just that Frog is so obviously on the hunt for a bride." She beamed. "I want a very stylish wedding gown from France. And a real wedding. None of this justice-of-the-peace stuff like you did."

Jade rolled her eyes. "I don't think you're going to get Frog. I think Suz has got her eyes—"

"Shh!" Betty said, her shushing startling both women. "Here, Daisy," she added, too brightly, "let me get you another cup of tea."

"Did you say Suz has her eyes on Frog?" Daisy looked positively electrified by this news. She hopped up from the table. "Thanks for the chat, girls. I have somewhere to be. By the way, congratulations on your wedding, Jade, though I don't think your marriage will last too long." She took one last piece of cake for the road. "I heard Ty telling a nurse that he thinks he's leaving the navy. Can you imagine? After he worked so hard to become a SEAL?" She shook her head. "It's a shame. But he says he needs to be here with his daughters and wife. I think no marriage lasts when one party has to give up everything to please the other partner, but what do I know?"

"Yes, what do you know, Daisy?" Betty demanded. "I don't recall you having a degree in marriage counseling."

Daisy laughed and waved as she headed out the back door. Jade sank into a seat.

"Don't listen to her," Betty cautioned. "She came in here to stir up trouble, and she has."

She certainly had. But Jade knew Daisy was telling the truth. If Ty had said he was planning to leave the navy, then he was. He wasn't the same man who had left BC. No doubt he felt turned inside out.

Jade's heart sank. It was too soon for him to make that decision. There were a lot of emotions flying around from the holiday homecoming, the wedding, finding out he was a father, finding out who his father was.

But Daisy was right: he'd worked too hard to become a SEAL. And Jade was the reason his life had totally blown up, from a too-talkative mother to secrets Jade herself had kept from him.

When he came home tonight, she was going to do her best to convince her handsome SEAL that everything was going to be just fine. He had to go back, had to follow his dream.

She intended to fight for her marriage.

Chapter Fifteen

A storm had turned loose inside Ty. Everything he'd once thought was the firm foundation of his life had been swept away.

He looked at his birth father lying on a bed in the hospital, giving commands to the nurses as if they had nothing better to do than be his personal servants. And of course, this was Robert Donovan, so who was going to tell him to pipe down?

"You need to pipe down," Ty said. "You don't need to always act like everywhere you go is part of your personal fiefdom. Your ticker is clearly telling you to chill out."

Robert stared at him, startled to hear a type of advice no one had dared give him before. "Why are you here?"

"Because." Ty sighed tiredly. "Because I hit you in your stupid mouth, because you had a small cardiac event and because you're my daughters' grandfather." He waved a hand dismissively. "Trust me, I don't want to be here any more than you want me to be."

"So now that you know you're related to money, you want to keep your eye on the golden goose?"

Ty looked at Robert with emotions bordering on disgust. "Really? That's your best shot? Always falling back on your big, fat wallet?"

Robert didn't look thrilled by Ty's lack of respect for his wallet. "You won't be in my will. And I expect some blood work to be done to prove this spurious claim your wife has come up with." He grunted, displeased by the entire turn of events. "In fact, I may have the nurses stick you while you're here."

"I think a simple swab will do," Ty said, "but knock yourself out. Look, just because we share a bloodline doesn't mean you're my father in any real sense of the word. So don't try to act like one at this late date."

Robert's bushy brows rose. "What does that mean, exactly? Are you turning your back on my money?"

"I couldn't care less if you have five dollars or five million. By an unfortunate turn of circumstance, your wife didn't like you enough to want a child with you." Ty felt that was a travesty. Still, Jade hadn't told him about his children, either. If he hadn't come home, he still wouldn't know. Might never have known. He drummed his fingers on the stiff metal-and-vinyl chair. This whole business with Jade trying to keep everything quiet was going to have to stop. Eve and Marie were his, and he wanted to know everything and anything about them. Maybe not with the attention to detail Sam apparently liked—down to the pooping schedule—but all the stuff that made a man a father, Ty planned to be in on.

"I'm staying in Bridesmaids Creek," he said. "Just to keep an eye on you, old man."

Robert's frowned at the disrespect he perceived from Ty's comment—and the adjective. "Old man! What son refers to his father that way?"

"I am not your son. Only in the blood sense. Please leave off all guilt trips. You're embarrassing yourself."

"Brave talk coming from a man on the government payroll." Robert sniffed. "See how much you have to live on and then I'll hear a different tune. You can't raise two babies and have a wife on a—"

"People do it all the time. Besides, I'm not exactly hurting financially."

"I'll buy your house, as I've offered to do many times. That should send your daughters to college."

Ty shook his head at Robert's endless calculations. "My dad sold you the land behind his house. You've had enough from the Spurlocks. You're not getting any more." He stood. "I have to go. Get on the mend, so I can give you hell."

"You know, Jade was awfully proud when you made it."

He felt a warm spot grow in his chest. "How do you know?"

"She went around town, telling everyone. She talked about you a lot."

This was news to him. Based on the amount of information he'd had from her while he was away, he'd have banked on the fact that she hadn't thought about him much. "Butt out, Robert. If I want a marriage counselor, I'll track one down. Just because we're unfortunately related doesn't mean I want any father-son chats, either."

"Yeah, well, I could use some assistance." Robert looked at him speculatively.

"With what?" Ty dreaded what he was about to hear. Donovan was as manipulative as the day was long. But he'd tried to coldcock the guy, so maybe he owed him a listen.

"Your sister—"

"Start over," Ty warned. "I'm serious. I want no discussion of us being a family. Do not try to tweak my heartstrings. As far as I'm concerned, I just learned that my family tree has a very undesirable root."

The older man shook his head. "I could use some help with my daughter."

"Can't help you."

"When I look at you," Robert said, drawing a deep breath, "I'm pretty proud."

"I don't care."

"What I'm saying is that I get why your mother… wasn't eager for me to raise a son. Raise you. Why she changed her mind about Daisy, I don't know." He sighed, sounding older than Ty had ever heard him sound. "Maybe she thought having a daughter would change me."

Ty remained silent, unmoved.

"Daisy is the apple of my eye. Having her just made me determined to conquer the world. You learn a little late in life that world-conquering is fine and dandy, but you really need to incorporate a few other elements into child rearing." He looked at Ty for a moment. "Your parents did a real fine job with you. Honestly, you're the kind of man any father would be proud to call his son."

Ty shook his head, not about to go there.

"So," Robert said heavily, "back to Daisy. She's already so much like me, and now that she knows she has a fractured family tree, she says she's on a mission to marry."

Ty snorted. "Sorry," he said, holding up a hand. "It's just that we're talking about Daisy."

"She says she's not going to let your daughters be the

talk of the town. That they're not going to be my only legacy, as far as grandchildren go."

"That ol' family tree thing biting you in the ass, huh? Kind of wish you'd read *The Book of Virtues* to her when she was growing up?"

Robert shrugged, closed his eyes. "I don't know what I would have done differently. Everything, I suppose. All I know is that now I don't want my kingdom fought over."

"No fighting here. I don't want a dime of your dirty money." Ty was incensed. "You've made that money off the backs of folks in this town that you either flat-out robbed by manipulation, or tried to crowd out with fear." He stood. "Your entire kingdom, as you call it, is very safe from the Spurlock clan. You have my word on it."

"But you'll help me with Daisy."

Ty hesitated. "What exactly do you want me to do? Daisy's hell on wheels. She's going to do precisely what she wants."

"I don't want her running off and marrying some joker who's after my money."

"You've been lording your money over this town for years. Where do you think someone could be found who wouldn't want in on a chunk of change?" Ty hated the fact that he was even thinking through Robert's dilemma. "What you need is Madame Matchmaker's expertise. Only problem is you've about ruined her and Phillipe's marriage by putting them under a load of financial pressure. You've wrecked his business in your pursuit of his little shop on the—" Ty stopped at the cagey look on Robert's face. "Oh, I get it. You've ticked off everyone in this town who has the resources to help you, and you want me to run interference. Hell, no. You made your bed, now lie in it."

Robert dolefully rubbed his chin where Ty had cold-cocked him, then pitifully massaged the area over his heart in a silent effort to stir up a little guilt.

"Oh, for crying out loud, Robert," Ty said, relenting slightly. "Who, exactly, do you have in mind for your wild-child daughter?"

"I was thinking," he replied enthusiastically, "maybe Sam or Frog, or Squint. You picked them, after all. You wouldn't have brought anyone to this town who wasn't honorable."

"You're asking me to hang one of my buddies out to dry."

Robert smiled. "There's gold at the end of the rainbow. Maybe one of your friends would think that's a plus."

"I thought you just said you didn't want anyone in the family who was after your dough."

"Those boys aren't from here. They know nothing about me, to speak of. And besides which, I'm not above trying to sweeten the pot. I just don't want anyone marrying my daughter who loves my money more than he loves her."

"You want the moon. What you're asking for is going to take matchmaking into a whole new gear." Ty edged to the door. "It would need skilled manipulation, with maybe even a little miracle or magic on the side."

"And you're the man who came up with the idea to bring a bunch of high-quality bachelors to town to marry off the local population of women, and improve the gene pool. All in an effort to save this town, namely from me." Robert grinned hugely. "I think I've come to the right place for what I need."

"This sucks," Ty said. "I'm not saying I'm helping you."

"If you quit the navy, it'll look like you're scared of me."

"Where did that come from?" Ty stared at the old man. "Does your mind never quit working?"

"Nope." He laughed, pleased. "I'm just saying, you need to remember that you're a hero for this town. Stay a hero. And find my daughter someone just like you. Maybe a little less stubborn, but otherwise the same."

"Stubborn comes with the brand. You don't get a SEAL without a heavy dose of stubborn, old man. Know what you're getting into."

Robert closed his eyes with a smile, and waved a hand majestically to dismiss him.

Ty rolled his eyes, still stunned that this ornery man could be his father, and departed, disgruntled beyond words.

All he wanted right now was Jade. It was his wedding day, for crying out loud, and he still hadn't had the kiss he'd been waiting for.

JADE GASPED WHEN the back door blew open and her husband walked in. "Ty! You scared me!"

"That is not what a man wants to hear when he returns to his bride's arms." He pulled her close, kissing her thoroughly, melting into her. "Oh, God, I missed this."

"I missed you, too."

She sounded breathless, and that was exactly how he wanted her. "Let's go have our honeymoon," Ty said.

"I think we should talk first, not that I want to talk on my wedding day." Jade sneaked her arms up his back, pressing him against her. "But in the spirit of the Christmas season, and in the spirit of being a totally honest, up-front bride, we probably should."

"And then we kiss. And other things."

She laughed. "Lots of other things. Betty's going to keep the babies, I've pumped some milk, and you and I are going away for the night."

"Where?" He didn't care, he just wanted to hold her.

"Your house for tonight. We'll stay close in case something comes up with the girls. Not that Mom isn't totally competent, but just in case. Then—" Jade kissed him more deeply, in a way that started his body sizzling "—Mom's wedding gift to us is a honeymoon in Paris."

"Paris?" He leaned back. "That's awesome. Expensive, but awesome."

Jade smiled, and he wanted to see that smile on her face always. "Apparently, Mom has saved up over the years for my wedding day. She wasn't counting on me having a home wedding in a post-maternity dress. She said the amount of money she'd put back for a wedding dress alone will cover the airfare."

"I love your mom." Ty was the luckiest man on the planet. "So what are we talking about?"

"Right now, we're taking our slices of wedding cake and going to your house. I'm all packed. Mom's fretting that I don't have a trousseau or a going-away outfit, and that no one threw birdseed or paper hearts at us, and I didn't toss a bouquet. Most of all, she's worried that I don't have a wedding negligee."

"It wouldn't be on you five seconds. Tell her it was good money saved."

"That's what I told her. But she's a mom. She's going to worry. Just like we're going to worry about our girls."

He actually had a lot of worries going on at the moment. "Let's get you on my white horse, then, and hit the honeymoon trail."

"But we talk first. We really, really have to talk, Ty."

He knew what this was all about. He would set her mind at ease, and then he was going to make love to her for the entire length of their honeymoon night. He picked up the honeymoon hamper Betty had thoughtfully packed.

"Let's go, bride. Talking isn't exactly my idea of foreplay."

She suddenly looked a little sad. "I know. But we really have to talk, because I promised you I wouldn't keep things from you anymore. And that's a promise I intend to keep."

It was that last bit that had Ty apprehensive. He didn't like his wife sounding so worried. He knew they needed to talk. But talking was something they should have done before, and she was right—she'd held things back from him. And he'd held things back from her.

He couldn't get a man-pass for that. He was just as guilty. So he took her to his house, opened the door and bent down to scoop her into his arms. "I'm a traditional guy," he said, and she kissed him.

"I like being in your arms. You can carry me over this or any other threshold."

That sounded better. More like she wasn't about to tell him to hit the road. He should be grateful if she wanted him to hit the road, because he was going to need a push to leave her behind.

"Wow," he said, and she got down from his arms, stunned by the transformation of his house.

"Yes, wow. Did you let the Christmas elves in?"

The Christmas tree alone was worthy of a Hollywood fairy tale. In fact, he couldn't remember how many years it had been since a tree had been in this house, and certainly never decked out like that. It was lovely, with silver and gold balls shining from every branch, reflecting the colors of the lights and the red velvet bows in every ornament. He didn't know much about decorating, but he could tell a lot of love had gone into the gift in their home.

"Changes our humble abode significantly, doesn't it?" Ty said.

"Humble? You call this house humble?" Jade laughed, and he put his arms around her, taking in the joy of sharing his first real Christmas tree with his brand-spanking-new wife.

"Oh, look!" Jade crossed to the fireplace mantel, admiring the handmade stockings. "We all have a stocking, including the girls."

He grinned hugely. "I probably have my old childhood stocking upstairs someplace, but I have no idea where to find it."

"I'll find it eventually. I'd like to see that." Jade smiled at him. "I remember when you were just a kid who got in lots of trouble. The sheriff had his hands full with you," she teased.

Ty felt slightly remorseful about the fact that he'd been a bit of a handful. "Yeah, I'd do a lot of things differently."

"I'm sorry, Ty. I shouldn't have said that." Jade hugged him. "Your father loved you so much."

"I know. He was a good man. If I'm half the dad he was—"

"You will be. Now come help me tear up this step."

"But we haven't finished the Christmas tour. And I'm not pulling up that stair. You did an awesome job repairing it." He had to remember he was the one who'd left his family secrets in her hands. Okay, he hadn't foreseen those secrets being spilled all over Bridesmaids Creek, but actually, it was better to get everything out in the open.

"Get your tool belt. We *are* tearing this stair apart. I'm not starting this marriage with any more skeletons waiting to jump out."

He did as she asked. "You're going to freak when you see the kitchen. By the holiday handiwork around here, I'm beginning to suspect your mother, Mackenzie, Suz, Cosette and Jane, at the minimum. They really went all out."

"That's what happens when you're the town's favorite son." Jade took the tool she wanted from his belt, then gazed at him thoughtfully. "You look really hot in that belt. Just so you know."

He grinned. "Just so you know, I'll be happy to put it on anytime for you. Let me do this. I'm the SEAL, remember? I'm supposed to be manly and tough."

"Go for it." Jade got down next to him, watching as he pried the stair apart. "I hope you're okay with this."

"I'm okay with it. I should have manned up in the first place." He pulled the board off the step, revealing the metal box, just where it had been before.

"It's not a matter of manning up. You were leaving for BUD/S. Wasn't your mind nice and clear when you left?"

"Not exactly." He stole a fast kiss from her. "I had a certain redhead on my mind all the time." Pulling the box free, he sat down with it. "You think this is necessary?"

"Absolutely." Jade nodded emphatically. "The more you know, the less Donovan can get to you."

"Yeah, about Donovan," Ty said. He looked at Jade. "He's decided he wants on Team Ty."

"Good. It's a step in the right direction. Of course, he's only doing it because of his granddaughters, but I'm okay with that. As long as you don't quit the SEALs, I'm good with learning to be a little nicer to Mr. Donovan. A *little*. And to not cut my sister-in-law's hair off anymore."

Ty looked at her, wondering if she knew exactly how much he loved her. Could it even be put into words? "I don't feel right about leaving you here holding the bag. It's not entirely fair if I leave you while I chase my dreams. You've got two new babies—"

"And that was *my* dream, if you recall." She touched his face. "Remember those days? Me worrying about my poor, underappreciated, untried ovary? You let me live my dream. I've got two darling babies to prove it."

"I told you that ovary was going to like my stuff."

She shook her head at his bragging, but he noted her lips were curved in a smile. "Read, Ty."

She sat next to him on the stair, putting her chin on his shoulder. God, that felt good. She felt good. He'd waited a long time for this. Ty hesitated before opening the envelope, just so he could enjoy the feeling of Jade supporting him a little longer.

"I can read it to you if you want," she said softly.

"I'm okay. I was just sitting here admiring your legs."

She kissed his cheek. "And I was admiring your hands. We can get on with a whole lot more than admiring if you do your book report, student."

"Yes, teacher." He pulled out the letter, reading fast, his heart hanging like a wild bird on the wind as he read his father's words to him. It was as if Ty could hear his voice, speaking his thoughts aloud. "Jeez," he said finally, his throat tight with emotion.

"Yeah. You weren't such a bad kid, after all." She kissed his cheek again, and Ty shook his head.

"Oh, I had my moments. But Dad was my best friend. He really was. I never felt like I'd let him down."

Ty picked up the box Robert Donovan's wife had left—he couldn't think of Honoria as his mother—and opened it. The Saint Michael medal gleamed, and he turned it over, seeing that she'd had his name engraved.

"Saint Michael is a strong protector, an archangel," Jade murmured against his shoulder. "You could think of Honoria's gift as a blessing that manifested in your life. You are strong, you are a protector." She kissed him. "I think she loved you a lot, Ty. From afar. And maybe she did the thing she knew was best by keeping you from Robert. Not to be mean, but you're certainly a good man. And he's not."

"Robert said something along the same lines." Not that he was anywhere near forgiving Robert for being a cretin, but Ty certainly didn't regret that his real family, the couple he would always remember when he thought of family, were the Spurlocks.

"Thank you for allowing me to share this moment with you," Jade said. "I was worried you'd never forgive me for the way everything got sprung on you."

He put everything back in the box, put the box in its

hiding place again. "It wouldn't be Bridesmaids Creek if everything wasn't sprung. Secrets don't come out gently and quietly around here. We do everything with dramatic intent. But what else would we expect from a town of carnies?"

She put her hand in his. "I think the box can go in our closet now, don't you?"

"You're right." He picked it up. "I'll fix the stair later. Right now, I have a wife to kiss."

"You'll note the mistletoe hanging from the arch," Jade said.

Ty shook his head, his whole world better with her in it. "It's sort of anticlimactic, don't you think? Kissing because of a pagan weed or whatever it is?"

"I think it's actually a fungus of sorts," Jade said.

"Which begs the question, what type of fungus would we hang to give us permission to make love?" He kissed her, then scooped her into his arms as she smiled at him. "I don't need a piece of mistletoe to kiss my Christmas bride."

"Good, because I plan on you kissing me every day," Jade said, "and frequently."

And those words were exactly what he wanted to hear. Ty Spurlock, U.S. Navy SEAL, husband, father and son, had finally come home for good. And nothing was going to ruin the best homecoming and Christmas ever, one he couldn't have dreamed up in his wildest delusional imaginings.

Wherever he was stationed, his heart would always be here. And there was nothing the Donovans or anyone else could do to ruin it.

He wasn't going to blow his second chance.

Chapter Sixteen

Daisy ripped up the main drag of Bridesmaids Creek, her gang of stooges following behind on their motorcycles. Since she'd discovered she wasn't an only child, she'd had very little to say to Ty.

Today, it seemed, she'd changed her game plan.

She stopped in front of Ty and Jade, her motorcycle roaring. "If it isn't my happily married big brother."

Ty winced. "Let's go easy on the family connections thing."

Jade glanced down at their daughters in the large-wheeled pram, making sure the blankets were covering them securely as they walked through Bridesmaids Creek, taking in the lovely holiday decorations.

"Here's the thing, Daze," Ty said, "you should start thinking about toning down your gig."

"My gig?" Daisy stared at him, her eyes piercing despite her helmet. She pulled it off, the chocolate locks flowing free. "My future husband is fine with my gig, thanks."

Ty stilled. "Future husband?"

"Yeah. Didn't you hear? I've got my sights set on Frog."

Jade glanced at him, startled. "Why Frog?" she asked Daisy.

"Suz didn't really have a chance, although secretly I think she's been setting her cap for him. And I think he'd be open to marriage. He protests a lot, but you know men. They change their minds pretty quickly when a baby comes on the scene, don't they, Jade?"

Ty shifted, knowing full well what was on Jade's mind. Her best friend was Mackenzie, and Mackenzie's little sister was Suz, and Suz had long had her eye on Frog.

Things always had to be complicated in BC.

"We should set up a Bridesmaids Creek swim for you," Ty said, feeling a bolt of inspiration hit him. "Or a Best Man's Fork run. That way, let the best man win." And he'd make sure Frog was pretty well out of commission before participating. Daisy winning Frog away from Suz would set up bad blood for years in BC.

"I'm not doing any of those silly things. It's just a bunch of fairy tales." Daisy shrugged, looking wildly beautiful in her skintight and somehow body-baring black catsuit. "You didn't. Why should I, brother?"

He hesitated. "I already had my lady." He hugged Jade close to him. "There was no reason to do any of the normal activities."

Daisy smiled. "If you don't, I don't. You can't say that your hurry-up wedding is a precursor to forever happiness. Jade just wanted a baby. Everyone knew it. The man was totally secondary. And you don't need a swim in the creek to know that."

Jade gasped. "That's a terrible thing to say, Daisy Donovan! Why are you bent on making trouble?" She hurried to pull the babies' tiny red knit caps down more fully over their ears, as if to protect them from the vile things their aunt was saying.

Ty took a deep breath. "Look. Life just happened for us. Let me set up a run or a swim for my little sister, okay?" He smiled winningly, figuring either one she chose, he could think up a way to have Squint win. Squint, at least, had half an eye for this completely wild woman who was now Ty's sister. Half an eye, he thought, that's just great. *He'd be better off blindfolded if he winds up married to Daisy.*

"I don't believe in the superstitions of BC," she said, not falling for his con. "Why are superstitions the mother's milk around here?"

"I don't know, but it's worked for every single person in Bridesmaids Creek," Jade said. "Except for Mackenzie's first marriage. She didn't do a swim, either. Maybe it was bad luck. Let Ty set something up for you."

"As I recall, Ty fixed her up with that first deadbeat." Daisy smirked. "My brother doesn't have the first clue about what makes a successful match. Or marriage."

Ty could tell they were in dangerous territory. Beside him, Jade had stiffened up, tense and unmoving. Any moment now, things could get ugly. More ugly than they were already. "You want the BC ways, Daze, you know you do."

"I just want a baby, Ty. Preferably a son. I don't need a big day of glory for that." She looked at the pram with a huge dose of loathing. "They really are cute little things. And if Jade can do it, so can I."

She tore off on her motorcycle, then looped back around to stop in front of them again. "I tell you what, brother. I'm pretty sure I see through your plan. You don't want me with Frog because of dear Suz."

He didn't say anything. Just watched his new sister carefully.

"I don't believe the creek is magical. I don't believe Best Man's Fork is, either. Frankly, I think Dad was better off when he wanted to mow this town down to the ground and bring in government offices. Make this the Washington, D.C., of Texas." Daisy looked at him speculatively. "But if you have such strong faith in the powers of our superstitions here, I'll let you set up a swim for me, or a run. I don't care which."

He nodded. "Good. I'll get right on it. Maybe just before Christmas."

"Oh, absolutely, just before Christmas." She grinned at him. "But I'll only agree to a run if Jade does, too."

Jade shook her head. "What will that prove?"

"It will prove that my brother married the right woman," Daisy said, her voice silky. "I mean, after all, it was such a hurry-up wedding, who can possibly know? Poor guy is home on leave, finds out his nighttime love had his children—what's he supposed to do?"

"That's disgusting, Daisy, even for you." Jade pushed the pram forward, moving off.

"She's scared to know the truth. When you've been born and raised in BC, these fairy tales mean everything. Me, I'm a transplant, as everyone always likes to remind me. But even I know when a marriage has started off on the wrong foot," Daisy told Ty.

He had started to deny it when his darling, hotheaded wife whirled around.

"A swim," Jade said. "All the guys will swim. And you'll eat your words, Daisy Donovan. I married the only man for me. I just hope Ty can talk one man into showing up for you. It's twenty-five degrees outside. It would take a really strong man to want to prove that he's the right man for you."

Daisy smiled at Ty. "Do not try to keep Frog from the competition. He's going to want in."

"How do you know?"

"Because Daddy's putting up a hundred thousand dollars for the winner. Every bachelor in town will want to swim." She laughed, gunned her bike and roared away, and Ty realized he'd been caught in a neatly set snare.

Crap-a-monkey. He didn't believe in superstitions, either. But he did believe in BC.

He certainly believed in his marriage.

So he'd swim. Like a SEAL that wanted everything to be just as magical as possible for the only woman he'd ever loved.

JADE WAS NERVOUS. She couldn't relax. Two days before Christmas, on Christmas Eve eve, the whole town was gathered on the banks of Bridesmaids Creek. She'd left the babies at home with Betty, because snow was falling and the forecast said it would snow all day.

"If you swim," she told Ty, "you're probably going to catch something besides me. Pneumonia."

"Not me. I've swum this creek many a time in the freezing cold." He zipped up a black wetsuit that fitted him quite nicely, Jade noticed.

Too nicely.

"I don't want any other women looking at you."

He laughed. "I'm going to be swimming so fast I'm going to be merely a shadow in the water. No worries."

She was worrying.

Ty came over to her, cradled her face between his palms. "I've got this. Everything's been taken care of."

"Meaning?" Jade wanted more reassurance than just confident words. Suz had been on the warpath for days, knowing exactly what Daisy was up to. Suz wasn't happy, either, that Frog had readily agreed to the swim.

She hadn't wanted to hear that any sane man would swim for a hundred thousand dollars. It had nothing to do with Frog having feelings for Daisy, because he didn't.

A knock at the front door caught their attention.

"Expecting someone?"

"No." Jade walked behind Ty to the front door of the house she was coming to love, where she felt very much at home with her husband.

Sheriff Dennis McAdams stood on the front porch.

"Hello, Sheriff. Come in," Ty said. "It's good to see you."

Dennis stepped inside. "You've really fixed the place up." He looked around, admiring the decorations.

"We didn't do this, actually. A team of elves decorated the place." Ty glanced at Jade, winking at her, which warmed her heart. "We think the ladies of the town sneaked in here, since Betty has access to Jade's key, but no one will admit to being our Secret Santas."

Dennis laughed. "Some secrets will stay secret, I guess."

"Let me get you a cup of tea, Sheriff." Jade turned toward the kitchen. "It's cold outside, and these guys are determined to swim."

"Believe me, I know. Daisy's gang started a bonfire in town. They're pretty liquored up, standing around, trying to stay warm." Dennis shook his head. "Somebody's going to drown if they keep drinking like college kids. Anyway, I can't stay, Jade, so I'll have to skip the tea. Thanks, though."

"What's on your mind, Sheriff?" Ty asked.

"Well, as you know, Robert Donovan is doing his best to turn over a new leaf. Just happens to be that leaves aren't that easy to turn." The lawman sighed, glanced around the cheery room as Jade leaned against Ty for support. She had the strangest feeling Dennis's mission today wasn't good news for them.

"Just so long as he decides to stay a changed man, that's fine by me," Ty said.

"The two deaths at the Haunted H—the one when your father was still…sheriff," Dennis said, carefully not using the word *alive,* "and the one earlier this year— Robert claims were accidental. But he did bring those men here for mischief. Both of them were meant to cause trouble. He's confessed to that."

"Awfully coincidental, don't you think? That both of his henchmen would die?" Ty asked.

"Donovan claims he just wants to start over. Wants a clean slate with everyone. Hence his confession." The sheriff zipped up his sheepskin jacket. "He's real worried that Daisy's gone over the edge. She liked being an only child. Hard to give up her kingdom, or princess-dom, I guess you'd say."

"Tough luck on that," Jade said, feeling a little guilt wash over her. Daisy still wouldn't know, and the town wouldn't be splitting apart, if she hadn't ever opened the Pandora's box under the stairs. And if she'd kept her mouth shut.

But it was too late for that.

"Confession's good for the soul, I guess. It wasn't

Robert's fault that the men died," the sheriff continued. "There's nothing I can charge him with."

"Criminal mischief?" Ty asked. "There has to be something."

"One charge is beyond the statute of limitations, and the other—hell, what would we prove?" The sheriff gazed at him. "Look, this might be a case where we realize Robert's trying to change, and we support him. For the sake of BC. Because honestly, I think Daisy's got more potential for mercilessness than her old man ever had."

"How do two men just randomly die at our haunted house?" Jade asked. "Something doesn't make sense. I know he was trying to destroy our dreams, and BC, but he's not telling you everything."

"Well, the first man had a serious heart condition, which Robert knew about. He chose him deliberately because of it. The man also needed money and was open to causing trouble—but it was just too much good fortune that he died on your father's watch. My guess is that both of these men were ill, and stress may have triggered their deaths. Unfortunate? Yes. Coincidental? Maybe. Partly. Robert chose men who would do his dirty deeds, and who had nothing to lose. The thing is, we'll never know for certain. The only thing you can do is not let it rule your life going forward." Dennis looked at Ty sympathetically.

"So two men die, and he blames it on Betty's toxic cocoa." Ty shook his head. "The man is a monster. He should be run out of town on a rail."

"He's admitted that he was behind the rumors that your father didn't look into the case seriously, and that his policies were flawed."

"Jackass," Ty said, and Jade could feel her husband breathing hard. "He destroyed my dad. His admission does my father little good now. Terence Spurlock died knowing this town had lost their trust in him."

"Yes." Dennis nodded. "I'm not saying you have to forgive Donovan for that. But forgiveness is just as meaningful for Bridesmaids Creek as it is for your life, Ty. You don't want to be imprisoned by the past forever." The sheriff sighed. "Donovan seems to be shedding his snakeskin and wants to make amends, ask forgiveness. He's started with his confession. He's also offered to set back half a million dollars for your girls, either for their education or their wedding, or—"

"We don't want a penny of Robert Donovan's money," Jade snapped. "In fact, I'm sick of hearing about it. And if you've come here on a mission of mercy from him, you're going back empty-handed."

Ty shrugged, proud of his wife's fire. "I'm afraid Jade's right."

"I totally understand. Think about it."

"So what did the second man really die of?" Jade demanded, unwilling to give much thought to the state of Robert Donovan's soul. "Since Robert's being so honest? Because I think he's lying through his teeth."

"According to him, and I've verified this through the autopsy results, that man had only a few months to live. Hence he was very open to the financial remuneration Robert offered him to come to the Hanging H that night. He, too, was supposed to cause a ruckus. Robert claims his goal was to set a small fire, maybe near the bunkhouse. To spook the customers and families, give the Haunted H a reputation for being an untrustworthy event."

Ty shook his head. "This is ridiculous. Donovan should be in jail, if for nothing else but being a creep and a son of a—"

"You tell Robert Donovan that he's footing the entire bill for the next ten years of haunted houses out at the Hanging H," Jade said, and Ty felt a surge of pride wash through him. "You tell him that he pays for ten years of Haunted H family gatherings, every single penny. And then maybe, just maybe, we'll think about whether we ever want to invite him to Christmas dinner!"

Ty glanced at her. Jade looked at him, feeling like a firecracker ready to explode.

"That's what this is all about, Ty. He's trying to clear the past so he can get forgiveness. So he can be with his granddaughters, and so he can be invited into our family."

"Is that likely?" Ty asked the sheriff. "Does Donovan actually think in terms of family?"

"My guess is yes. At least that's what it sounded like to me. He's an old man who's done a lot of wrong. It's time for him to come clean. And he's a smart man. He knows that eventually skeletons pop out of closets."

"Tell me about it," Ty said.

Jade grabbed her coat. "And he cancels every single sale and contract he may be negotiating, or may have negotiated, with any entity to come here, whether it be government or not. He stops trying to bulldoze people out of their homes and their businesses, and most especially, he leaves Phillipe and Cosette Lafleur alone." Jade buttoned her red coat and slipped on some white mittens, looking very Christmassy and darling to Ty. Sexy, and somehow like a Christmas angel, too.

"And all business decisions he makes concerning

sales, any sales of any property, have to go through the town council, which consists of Ty or myself, and Cosette, Phillipe, Jane Chatham and her husband, Ralph, Betty, Mackenzie and Justin Morant, as well as yourself, Sheriff. Those are my conditions. He'll have to take it or leave it."

Jade glanced at the two men, who seemed disinclined to argue with her, or tell her that she was asking for the moon.

"If he wants to see his granddaughters, and hold them, and be part of their lives. If he wants to darken the door of this home at Christmas or any other time, that's my final and only offer. And now, if you gentlemen will excuse me, I'm off to man the hot-cocoa stand at the creek. My husband has a race to win for me today." She rose on her tiptoes to kiss her hunky husband goodbye. "I love you. Swim like Flipper."

He grinned. Time and two babies had not knocked one ounce of sass out of his lovely redhead. "See you at the finish line, gorgeous."

Jade went out, bundled to the max, her red-and-white scarf flying in the breeze.

"I guess you know that she's the only woman who could have tamed your heart," Dennis observed. "She's got a helluva lot of spunk."

Ty just smiled hugely.

Chapter Seventeen

To say that Ty swam like seven devils were after him was no understatement. He felt awesome, as if he was back in BUD/S, pitting himself against himself, the weather and all the men who had the same goal he did—to be the very best.

He won, easily. Way ahead of the pack. Climbed out of the frigid water to be rewarded by his wife throwing herself into his arms.

"Superstition or not," he said, gasping for air, "I know I'm married to the only woman who is my better half. My significant other. The apple of my eye," he announced to the cheering crowd. "The milk in my cereal, the cherry on my pie. Long live Bridesmaids Creek!"

Jade laughed, kissing him. "You'd better sit down, husband, and drink some cocoa. You sound a little punchy. A little bit like you've been to Daisy's bonfire and gotten into the hooch."

"Yeah, but it was romantic," he said, collapsing on the bench where she led him. "Wasn't it?"

She smiled and put a warm blanket around him. "Very romantic. Silly, but romantic. When you catch your breath, there are warm, dry clothes waiting in your truck."

Clothes could wait. He got to his feet, lumbered to the side of the creek to see how the other fellows were doing. How fast could men swim for a hundred thousand dollars?

Daisy stood on the bank, wearing a drop-dead black cashmere pantsuit that clung to her every curve. She had on black boots, and her long hair whipped around as she cheered the swimmers on.

It looked as if Squint was going to win. Ty breathed a sigh of relief. The Plan was, as he'd instructed his brothers, that all three of them would swim faster than Daisy's gang—but then, at the last second, Squint was to touch the bank first. Frog and Sam were to cede the lead, though discreetly, thereby throwing the race to their friend.

The three would split the money, according to the terms Ty set forth for his brothers.

They'd readily agreed. They'd had to. It was his sister, he'd pointed out, his father-in-law's money, and Ty planned to beat their heads in if they didn't do exactly what he told them.

Squint was the fall guy, the sacrificial lamb, because he actually had, as Ty had pointed out with no thought to a pun, half an eye for Ty's dangerous sister. And Squint wasn't as easygoing as Frog. Frog wasn't capable of handling a woman like Daisy—she'd run all over him.

"Swim, Squint!" Ty yelled, unable to help himself. He'd known he'd be far in front of his brothers, but they seemed to be swimming slowly, by his calculations.

Even retired SEALs should be in reasonable shape.

To his shock, Daisy's gang began to pull in front. Something was terribly wrong. His brothers were slowing to a crawl.

"What's happening?" Jade asked. "Does something seem not right to you?"

He shook his head, his jaw dropping when all of a sudden, Frog touched first and jumped out of the water, dripping and gasping from the last-ditch effort he'd put forth.

Daisy's gang came in second, third, fourth, fifth and sixth.

Sam came in seventh. And Squint—he was dead last.

And everyone knew what coming in last meant.

It meant he didn't have a chance in hell of a happy marriage—or any marriage at all—in Bridesmaids Creek.

"It doesn't matter," Jade said as they went upstairs to their bedroom that night. Ty let his bride tuck him into bed, insisting he get under a pile of blankets. She was just certain he'd caught a chill.

Ty had never felt better. But he certainly wasn't opposed to letting his wife warm him up. She had that look on her face, as if she was in the mood for some Christmas fun, and he smiled. This was the real prize, the real win, being in bed with his beautiful wife, with the babies tucked into the nursery down the hall. The tree was twinkling downstairs, and so many presents billowed out from under it that it was clear Santa had arrived early.

Santa SEAL. "Come here, wife."

She snuggled up to him, warming him the way he'd known she would. "It's just a race in a pond, a fund-raiser for our small town. Deep inside, you know that, Ty."

"You're trying to say it doesn't matter that somehow Squint didn't win. How does Squint suddenly get a leg cramp? He knows better than to let pain be his guide!

What a wienie." Ty was outraged by his friend's sudden weakness. "I think he threw the race on purpose."

"We'll never know." She kissed Ty, trailing her fingers along his jaw. "Daisy gigged herself a Frog, and he claims he had to take one for the team because he could tell that Sam and Squint were struggling."

"I don't believe a word of it. I think Frog's competitive side kicked in."

"The money helped his time, no doubt." Jade laughed. "And although Suz is beside herself, it's for them to straighten out. But I have a question. Why did you do the swim? Truthfully? You didn't have to."

"For the traditional reasons, and then my own personal reason." He thought he felt a bit of breast underneath the frilly white gown Jade wore, and it was making it hard to concentrate on what was a very important conversation. "I wanted you to know that I wanted to win you. I knew those guys couldn't beat me. I'm in shape, and clearly, they're not."

"Frog, Squint and Sam donated their winnings to the BC hospital. What do you think about that?"

He kissed her fingertips, loving every minute he got to spend holding her. "That I picked them because I knew they were good men. So I expected nothing less from the three wild boys. They get a little crazy on occasion—"

"And that's why we love them. All of you."

Her hand drifted lower to his abdomen, her fingers moving over his muscles, which he wasn't too proud to admit were washboard tight, thanks to the SEALs. "You're going to be all right with being a navy wife?"

"You mean, with you being gone all the time?" Jade nipped his shoulder lightly. "I plan to give you plenty to remember while you're gone. So, about these reasons."

He smiled at his wife's curiosity. "I wanted you to know that I believe in us. That I trust you. All that bit about you ruining my trust because you didn't tell me about the babies, and other things, is something that belongs in the past. Buried." He kissed her, loving how she melted against him. "Some things *can* stay buried in BC."

Jade looked up at him. "You mean that, don't you?"

"Of course I do. Didn't I just prove it? I've still got the shivers that back up my words," he said, fibbing a bit. "You can get a lot closer. It'll help me warm up."

He put her on top of him, and she kissed his lips, bringing him a hot, sexy rush. "And the other reasons?"

He looked at Jade, the woman he'd dreamed of for so long. "Why else does a man rise to meet a challenge? I wanted you to have your own memory to brag about. And I believe that people will be talking about today's race for a long time to come."

He stroked the burgundy-red hair that stayed aflame even in his dreams. "I told you, I'm a traditional guy. I go by a plan, although I'm learning that sometimes the plan goes rogue, which, when it comes to you and my daughters, is okay. Redheaded-and-rogue suits me fine. And I love you. Like crazy."

"I love you, too." She smiled down at him. "Merry Christmas, my sexy SEAL."

He grinned and pulled Jade against his chest, holding her close to his heart. It *was* a very merry Christmas, and as Christmases usually went in Bridesmaids Creek, it was magical.

* * * * *

14_ST_3

MILLS & BOON®

Want to get more from Mills & Boon?

Here's what's available to you if you join the exclusive **Mills & Boon eBook Club** today:

- ✦ *Convenience – choose your books each month*
- ✦ *Exclusive – receive your books a month before anywhere else*
- ✦ *Flexibility – change your subscription at any time*
- ✦ *Variety – gain access to eBook-only series*
- ✦ *Value – subscriptions from just £1.99 a month*

So visit **www.millsandboon.co.uk/esubs** today to be a part of this exclusive eBook Club!